Decker

An Eidolon Black Ops Novel: Book 10

Maddie Wade

Preface

Decker:
An Eidolon Black Ops Novel: Book 10
By Maddie Wade

Published by Maddie Wade
Copyright © October 2021

Cover: Envy Creative Designs
Editing: Black Opal Editing
Formatting: Black Opal Editing

Acknowledgments

I am so lucky to have such an amazing team around me without which I could never bring my books to life. I am so grateful to have you in my life, you are more than friends you are so essential to my life.

My wonderful beta team, Greta, and Deanna who are brutally honest and beautifully kind. If it is rubbish you tell me, it is and if you love it you are effusive. Your support means so much o me.

My editing team—Linda and Dee at Black Opal Editing. Linda is so patient, she is so much more than an editor, she is a teacher and friend.

Thank you to my group Maddie's Minxes, your support and love for Fortis, Eidolon, Ryoshi, and all the books I write is so important to me. Special thanks to Rowena, Tracey, Faith, Rachel, Carolyn, Kellie, Maria, Greta, Deanna, Sharon, Becky, Vicky, and Linda L for making the group such a friendly place to be.

My Arc Team for not keeping me on edge too long while I wait for feedback.

Lastly and most importantly thank you to my readers who have embraced my books so wholeheartedly and shown a love for the stories in my head. To hear you say that you see my characters as family makes me so humble and proud. I hope you enjoy Decker and Savannah's story as much as I did.

Cover: Envy Designs

Editing: Black Opal Editing

To all those people who are grieving the loss of a loved one.
This is for your strength and courage.

Prologue

"Congratulations, Deck, we never would've caught that bastard without you."

Mark Decker grinned at Scott Silverman as they made their way back to their vehicles parked along the sidewalk. They'd just taken down a huge sex trafficking ring that until now had been thriving in New York City.

"It wasn't all me, you know."

Scott punched him lightly on the arm. "Don't be modest, you're on the fast track now, my friend. After that, the world is your oyster. You can have your pick of assignments."

"Maybe, but I love New York. It's so alive, so full of energy." He considered his hometown not two hours' drive from here and yet it had none of the vibrancy he loved. A tiny smidge of guilt assailed him, taking the shine off his win when he thought of his wife, Susan. He loved her beyond anything, apart from his son and the daughter she was expecting in just a few short weeks. They meant everything to him and the fact he knew deep down she hated it here marred the enjoyment.

He'd promised her when they'd moved that it would only be for a few years until he was established, and she knew it was his dream job. She was the best woman alive, and he loved her to bits. From the first second he'd laid eyes on her when she started at his school freshmen year, he'd been a goner.

With her long blonde hair, hazel eyes and a sweetness that was so ingrained in her, she was his polar opposite. All she'd ever wanted was to be a mother, and she was the best mother to their son, Milo. At three, he had the sweetest personality; funny, clever, and loving but he also had a stubborn streak, which was all him.

"Maybe a change would be good though." He pulled open the door, a sense of rightness that he was going to move his family closer to the suburbs where Susan would be happier and Milo and their unborn daughter, who they'd yet to meet or name, could thrive. This was where his job was, but his family needed space to grow and feel safe and he, more than anyone, knew the dangers of the city.

The noise from the morning rush hour was dying down and he moved to his desk and sat heavily as he took out his phone to call Susan and tell her of his decision. It rang out and he hung up without leaving a message. She was most likely walking Milo into pre-school. The drop-off line wasn't something she liked and insisted on walking him inside. He smiled as he remembered her rant about it last week and how he'd silenced her with a kiss that had ended up with him on his knees between her legs.

Susan wasn't the most adventurous, but he could always coax a response from her. They had a good life, a good marriage, and if the sex was a little uninspired that was fine. He enjoyed it and he didn't need anything else.

Decker set about writing up the report from that morning's incident and was just finishing up when his supervisor walked toward him. This was it; he was going to get a big slap on the back and the praise he'd earned with tireless hours spent hunting these bastards.

"Mark, can I have a word in my office please?"

Decker paused, brushing the wrinkles out of his jacket as he stood, not liking the serious tone or the fact he wouldn't make eye contact.

"Sure."

Decker stepped inside and heard the door close behind him.

"Take a seat, Mark."

Decker did as he was asked but now his gut was churning, his hands tingling with what felt like a warning, and his flight or fight response was kicking in, as if he knew he didn't want to hear what was about to be said.

His boss, Special Agent in Charge Nolan Freeman, sat behind his large glass desk and clasped his fingers in a pyramid. He glanced up and locked gazes with him and Decker felt the bottom of his world fall out at Freeman's words. "Mark, there's no easy way to say this, but Susan and Milo were in a car accident at eight-thirty this morning. Their car was t-boned by a delivery truck."

Decker tried to breathe through his nose as his vision swam and his mind reeled as if trying to process the unimaginable.

"No." The chair fell back as he stood quickly. "I have to see them, they need me." He ran a hand through his hair as he backed toward the door. Freeman stood and came toward him slowly. "Which hospital?"

"Mark!"

"Which fucking hospital?" he screamed knowing he was acting irrationally.

"Mark!"

Freeman gripped his upper arms, the words stern but in some sick way full of sympathy, which he couldn't take. He began to shake his head not wanting to hear any more. "No, don't say it. Please don't say it."

"I'm so sorry, Mark. They were both killed and so was the baby. I'm so incredibly sorry."

Decker slumped into the chair, the room around him fading as pain, the likes of which he'd never felt, carved a hole in his chest. A loud keening sound hit his ears and he realised it was him as he rocked back on the chair, arms across his middle as if trying to hold himself from falling apart. How was it possible to live through this amount of pain? How would he live without the sweet smile of his son? How would he live without hearing Susan laugh at his terrible jokes?

"I need to see them."

Freeman pursed his lips and Decker looked away. "I'll get someone to take you to the hospital. You'll need to formally identify them."

Suddenly the urge to be with his family, to see them for himself was overwhelming. Perhaps this was a terrible mistake, and Susan would waddle walk towards him, her big hazel eyes brimming with love, and they'd laugh at this silly mistake.

Thirty minutes later any hope he'd held onto was dashed as he looked down at the bodies of his wife and son laid out side by side in the hospital mortuary. He stroked her face, held his son's cold hand, and sobbed for the loss, knowing he'd never feel whole again. That he'd live what life he had left with a huge, gaping festering wound in his chest and if he were lucky, it would kill him, and he could join the people he loved.

He laid his head on her still round belly and prayed for a sign that this was all just a nightmare. That he'd wake up and Milo would jump on him and curl his tiny arms around his neck and ask him to play soccer, but the nightmare never ended.

"I'm so sorry, Susie. This should be me. I should be the one lying here, not you. If I'd just stayed home and done the school run like you'd asked, but I put my job first." He kept talking to her and to his son and the daughter he'd never hold and, the entire time, his friend Scott Silverman, who'd driven him to the hospital, stood and waited.

The coming days were a blur of people, and names, of softly spoken words of condolence. Yet, he could hardly remember any of it. He was too numb to feel after the initial shock. He barely ate or drank, constant nausea making food seem repulsive. He slept in the bed he'd shared with his wife, her scent still on the pillow and wished he was dead.

The day of the funeral arrived, and Decker dragged himself from his pit of despair and showered, letting his tears mingle with the water he'd turned hot enough to scorch his skin in an attempt to feel something other than this overwhelming pain. Emptiness knotted like a cramp in his gut and his body seemed to weigh a ton as grief bore down on him. He dressed in a black suit with a vest and the blue silk tie Susie had brought for him last Christmas. It felt like armour, like he was putting on a show, as if something as simple as a wardrobe change could help.

Glancing in the full-length wardrobe mirror, he saw a man who'd aged ten years. Not a twenty-seven-year-old man in his prime but one who was haunted, his life over for all intents and purposes. He wished again that he'd been the one to die and not his beautiful family.

A slight knock on the door had him turning to see Scott waiting for him. "You ready?"

Decker shook his head, the words stuck in his throat. He'd never be ready to say goodbye to them, but he had no choice. "No, but I have to."

Scott put his hands in his pockets and looked at the floor. Nobody knew what to say to him and he got that, but the silence was almost as bad.

The church in the small hometown where they'd grown up was filled with family and friends. Susan's mother and father met him, and they hugged, each locked in their own hell of grief and pain. Decker straightened and swallowed, hiding behind a feigned composure as he shook hands and spoke nonsensical words with well-wishers and listened to shared memories of Susan and Milo, but hardly any of it went into his brain. Most swirled around before dissipating into the air, forgotten on the winds of time just as they'd be nothing but a sad memory for some. Not for him. He'd never forget them; he'd lock away his memories so time couldn't dull them and face the world for what was left of his life with no emotion or love in it.

He fingered the soft green dinosaur in his hands as he moved to the front of the church and the open caskets that he hadn't wanted but had gone along with for her family's sake. Milo's tattered dinosaur teddy had become his most treasured possession since their deaths, or at least until now and then he gently kissed his son's cold skin and placed the soft toy beside him.

"Sleep well, my baby boy. Daddy loves you so much and I'll see you again one day."

He did the same with Susan, his hand resting lightly on the still stomach where their daughter had lived and died. "I'm sorry, baby. I should've protected you. I hope one day you forgive me."

The following weeks were a blur of whiskey induced grief where he was barely sober most of the time and knew he was hurting the people who cared about him. He got up, went to work, hardly spoke, didn't really interact but did his job, hiding behind the suit that seemed to scream 'hands-off'. His colleagues and friends tried to reach him, and, in some ways, he felt bad for what he was putting them through, but he just wanted to be gone. To leave this world full of pain and fear and be with his family.

He sat in his home surrounded by reminders of his failures and looked at the service pistol on the coffee table. One moment was all it would take to end it all and be with them again. One jerk of his finger on the trigger and it would be over. He held the weapon in his hands and let his brain remember all the small inconsequential interactions he'd had with his family and missed them more, but it was those memories and the ringing of the doorbell that saved him. He couldn't throw away the life he'd been gifted so selfishly. He'd honour his family by being the best person he could be. He let Scott into the house and knew he'd seen the whiskey and gun on the coffee table and winced as he sat beside him.

"This isn't the answer, man."

"I know, I just realised that." His voice was thick with tears, and he felt shame for breaking down again.

"I just miss them so fucking much."

Scott pulled him in for a hug and Decker leaned on his friend and cried. He sniffed and swiped his sleeve across his burning eyes.

"You need a change of scenery. To get out and away from the memories before you drown."

"I know and I was offered a job in the UK with a new company. I would've turned it down before but now I think it's just what I need."

Scott glanced sideways at him. "You'd leave the FBI?"

"Yes, I'll still be a profiler but with a private company and not with the FBI."

"It might be what you need to heal."

Decker shook his head. "I don't think you heal from this. You just learn to live with the pain and hope it doesn't kill you."

Scott nodded slowly and moved to the kitchen. He went through the cupboards and found a glass before joining him on the couch. He poured them both a glass of whiskey, which soured in Decker's gut. "To fresh starts."

"To fresh starts."

Eight weeks later, Decker was on a plane watching the New York skyline disappear as he headed for a new start without the loves of his life, his heart forever left in the Big Apple.

Chapter One

Savannah smiled to herself as she watched Astrid and Jack dance, surrounded by their friends and family, especially Adeline and Lopez, who after a very rough start had found love. It filled her bruised heart with hope that maybe one day she'd find that same kind of love. Not the fake façade her ex-husband had offered her before deciding monogamy wasn't for him and forgetting to let her know.

Leaning against the wall of the beautiful castle, a sigh escaped her as she sipped on her champagne. It had been a day of surprises, especially as the actual Queen had attended the ceremony, and her now friend and former patient, Adeline, getting a surprise proposal followed by a dance from Jack and his friends that had finished off a wonderful day.

She felt him before she saw him. Something about the cool, clever, handsome profiler who seemed to dislike her immensely rattled her. Perhaps because it was unusual for someone to dislike her so much when she'd done nothing wrong to them that she was aware of, or maybe it was because she found him so damned attractive that her heart sped up at the sight of him, despite the unnecessary barbs he threw her way.

Savannah refused to turn and acknowledge his presence. She was there first and if he wanted to disturb her peace then he could make the first move at conversation.

"I suppose you buy into all this happily ever after nonsense too?"

Savannah hid the smile at her tiny victory and turned, her eyebrow raised in question. "Nonsense?"

"That mystical happy ever after."

Savannah ran a critical eye over Mark Decker, who looked as delectably unattainable as ever in his three-piece grey suit that fit like it was made for him, which it most likely was. He was beyond hand-some, tall, his dark hair swept back from his forehead, and if she guessed correctly, it had a slight wave in it. Deep brown eyes that seemed to hold a wealth of secrets, long, inky black lashes and high cheekbones that complimented a jaw cut from marble, which was probably cut from the same template that had been used on Michelangelo's David.

Savannah had no idea why he was so damn off with her when he was perfectly delightful with everyone else. Especially when his eyes swept over her from head to toe, a hot look of desire in them. It gave her a giddy feeling to be wanted by him when it was clear he didn't want to want her.

Turning away and back to the scene on the dance floor, she cocked her head at his question. Watching the love before her it was hard to understand how he could think that way.

Looking up at him again she was struck by how tall he was. She was five feet seven so by no means short, but he towered over her, his shoulders wide and powerful. She knew he was built, had seen him after a training session in the gym at his work and still had fantasies about it.

He continued to watch the floor not looking at her.

"I think the people in front of us are proof it's real, Mark."

She saw his jaw flex and wondered what she'd said this time to upset him.

"It never lasts, that's the problem with perfection."

"I don't think any of them would say it's perfect, but it's perfect for them and that's what counts. Have you never been in love, Mark?" She didn't know what made her ask the question, whether it was the champagne or the atmosphere, but he almost winced at her words, and she knew she'd hit a tender spot.

"Once."

He said no more, and she regretted asking, knowing she'd caused him pain and that had never been her plan. She was a healer at heart, always had been, and still was, her goal always to help not harm.

"Tell me, Dr Sankey, do you get a kick out of poking your nose in where it's not wanted?"

Savannah sucked in a breath at the hurtful comment she knew was said for that very reason. Mark Decker was acting like a wounded bear and lashing out. As much as she wanted to be the bigger person, she wouldn't be an emotional punching bag for him or anyone else.

"I think this little discussion, if you can call it that, is over. If you'll excuse me, I need some air." Without waiting for his reply, she pulled her wrap tighter around her shoulders and walked onto the balcony behind her, leaving Mark Decker to his own misery.

The night was clear, the sky obsidian with millions of stars twinkling above her. Savannah sucked in a breath of the cool, fresh air and let it out slowly. She loved nights like this when it felt like the sky was the limit and endless possibilities were laid out. Seeing the love surrounding her today reminded her of her own solitary existence.

She'd put everything into her mission to become the best neurosurgeon she could be, and had made so many sacrifices, none of which she regretted. Her marriage had been a sham from the very beginning. Andy Farr was one of the top neurosurgeons in the country. He was also arrogant, conceited, and in the beginning, charming. She'd mistaken his late nights and missed dinners as a commitment to his job. God knew she was the same but while she was working, he was screwing around.

She gave a shake of her head, banishing thoughts of the man who'd broken her heart. He didn't deserve the head room she was giving him. It was almost two years now and their divorce had been finalised the previous week. Andy had been hell-bent on winning her back, blocking the divorce at every turn until he'd gotten one of the scrub nurses pregnant and she'd forced his hand. Savannah actually felt sorry for her. Andy would never stay faithful, and she knew now what she'd thought was love was more hero worship. For all his faults, and there were many, he was a wonderful surgeon.

Savannah felt movement behind her and knew who it was without turning around. His cologne was distinctive to him, and she hated the fact she could pick it out after he'd been such a jerk to her before. She turned to leave, not wanting another sparring session with Mark Decker, and avoided eye contact.

"Don't go." A firm hand landed on her forearm, stopping her momentum and she glanced up at him. He really was sinfully handsome yet so distant and guarded. "Please. I'm sorry I was rude to you earlier."

Her lips twitched with a smile, knowing that the apology must have cost him. He didn't strike her as a man who easily admitted when he was wrong. No, Mark Decker was a man with exacting standards for himself and those around him. Savannah resumed her place, looking out over the beautifully lit gardens of the Castle with the stars above and the backdrop of laughter and music coming from behind them.

Savannah sipped her champagne and angled slightly towards Mark. He was looking out over the landscape, and it gave her a moment to study the sexy yet unreadable man, to wonder what made him the person he was, what secrets he held. He looked so proud and strong, like a warrior of old and she knew he must have scars inside to have earned the pain she saw deep within him. His dark hair was combed perfectly, and she had the urge to run her fingers through it and mess him up a bit, just to see his reaction. The image of him sweaty and unguarded the one time she'd seen him with his friends popped into her thoughts, and she wondered what kind of woman would be able to make a man like him love her and what had happened to make him so cold.

"Why don't you like me?"

Mark angled his body to her, one perfectly arched brow raised in question. "I don't dislike you. I hardly know you."

"No, you don't, yet I still get the feeling I've done something to annoy you and I don't know what it is."

"You haven't done anything to *annoy me* as you put it, Dr Sankey."

Savannah snorted and rolled her eyes. "If you say so."

"What does that mean?"

Savannah seemed to have his full attention as he turned more towards her. "You're snide, cold, and rude. You argued with every assessment I made on Adeline even though I'm a leading expert in my field, and you've made it more than clear that you can't stand being around me."

"Seems like you've given this a lot of thought."

Savannah shrugged. "People generally like me, so when someone doesn't, it bugs me."

Mark stepped closer, his eyes travelling over her face in a slow perusal that had her breath hitching and her body tingling. He lifted one hand from his pocket and curled a finger around a strand of her long hair, which she'd left down to hang in waves over her shoulders for once.

"You have this all wrong, Dr Sankey. I do like you." He frowned as he twirled her hair between strong tanned fingers. "You have the prettiest eyes."

His compliment caught her off guard and she gasped. Decker dipped his head slowly and she closed her eyes waiting for his kiss, her heart pounding in her chest. She'd never wanted a kiss more than she did this one.

His lips brushed hers gently, almost a whisper and then it was like fire raged through her and she gripped the lapels of his jacket, wanting him closer as his lips, firm and sure, drugged her. Her sigh allowed him to move his tongue along her bottom lip, his hands on her hips now pulling her closer to his heated body.

It was everything a first kiss should be, confident, powerful, and mind-blowing. Her body was alight with desire for him, her hands wanting to feel his skin beneath her fingers. To see if he was as warm as she imagined and if his body was as hard as the glimpses of muscle had hinted at.

"Deck! Oh, shit. Sorry."

Decker pulled abruptly away as if she'd scalded him and looked at her with shock and distaste, putting distance between them as he turned to Waggs, who was looking sheepish as he stood at the door to the balcony.

"What can I do for you, Waggs?"

Was she imagining it or was his voice deeper and more gravelly than before? It was hard to tell with his stiff back to her.

"Sorry to interrupt, but Jack wants a quick word."

Humiliation slammed through Savannah as he ignored her as if what they'd shared meant nothing, worse, was a mistake.

"No interruption. I was just placating Dr Sankey's delicate ego."

Savannah felt molten heat move through her veins, this time fury and anger replacing the embarrassment from seconds before. "You bastard."

Savannah pulled the shawl tighter around her shoulders and moved through the balcony door with her head held high as she nodded at Waggs, who looked unhappy. She made it inside and slouched against the frame to catch her breath and calm her anger. Hot tears of shame over falling for his charm and sexual manipulation burned her eyes.

"Fucking hell, Deck. That was a dick thing to do."

She could hear Waggs speaking through the door but didn't stop to listen. She had no interest in what Mark Decker had to say. She was done with men who didn't respect her or value her. It was time to go home to her gorgeous three bedroom detached house and snuggle in her bed with a good book.

Savannah took a taxi home. She'd had too much to drink to drive and, having seen the devastation alcohol and driving could have on the brain, she never took the chance. As she paid the driver and stepped out of the cab, the nude heels that were much higher than the usual crocs she wore for work, pinched. They looked great, and her legs looked a mile long in them and they gave her ass some sway, but she'd be so glad to kick them off. As she neared the door, her steps faltered. Across her front door in bright red paint was the word 'murderer'. It seemed like her day wouldn't be getting any better from this point on.

Chapter Two

"**W**hat the hell, Deck? I know you can be direct but you're not usually an asshole about it." Decker looked at his friend and saw the censure in his gaze. Regret hit him over the way he'd treated Savannah. He'd been cruel and dismissive, and it was unfair. The truth was she'd done nothing at all to court his ire.

She was smart and kind and damn beautiful, and that was the crux of the problem. He liked her way more than he felt comfortable with. From the second he'd seen her, she'd instigated a pull in him like he'd never felt before and he didn't like it one bit. He saw the hurt on her face when he'd sniped at her not once but twice today and shame at his own conduct made him drop his friends gaze and look away.

"I know. I was a dick and I'll apologise."

Waggs brushed his hand over his jaw and shook his head. "You'd better. Astrid and Adeline will have your balls in a vice if you upset their friend."

The thought of either of those women upset or disappointed in him grated. He wasn't frightened of them, but he hated the idea of making them angry. The last ten years had been tough, but Eidolon had saved him. As Eidolon had grown as each man met their soul-mate, and so had his extended family. None of it stopped him from missing his wife and son, or the daughter he'd never had the pleasure of holding for even a second. He'd carry that wound to the grave, but it had made everything more bearable.

"You're right. I'm gonna see if I can find her now and say sorry for being a dick."

"Good."

Decker remembered then that Waggs had been looking for him. "What did Jack need?"

Waggs gave a wry smile. "He's just micromanaging and stressing about being away for three weeks. Go. I'll tell him we have it under control."

"Cheers, man." Deck swept past Waggs, his eyes moving over the swathe of people dancing and having fun, looking for a head of golden-brown hair that hung in beachy waves over graceful shoulders. He moved through the guests, resisting Bebe and Laverne's attempts to drag him onto the dance floor.

He stopped beside Adeline and Lopez, who were talking to Skye and Nate from the Fortis crew. "Have you seen Savannah?"

Adeline frowned at his question "What did you do?"

Decker gritted his jaw at the insinuation. "Why would you assume I've done anything?"

"Oh, I don't know. Perhaps because you're a douche bag every time you speak to her."

Decker reared back in surprise. Yes, he could be terse and perhaps a little stand-offish, but he'd never been cruel until tonight and he was trying to fix that if only people would get out of his damn way.

"I'm not in any way horrible to her." He refused to use the word douchebag in any way.

Adeline rolled her eyes. "Whatever you say, Deck. Anyway, she left. You just missed her."

Decker fought the sigh of frustration and thanked Adeline, but her words played on his mind and on a whim, he decided he needed to speak to Savannah and find out if he'd been an asshole to her. It was never his intention, but he wasn't himself around her, she sparked too much emotion. Lust he could handle. He hadn't been celibate the last ten years but with her it would never be just sex. Women like her always wanted more —the fairy-tale, the happy ending, and he just didn't have that in him anymore. That had died with his family, but he liked Savannah, had found her witty and interesting the times he'd been around her, and he didn't like the idea of her upset with him.

He jogged to his car wishing he had his bike instead, the freedom and peace he found on the machine soothing his soul. Instead, he jumped into his Mercedes C-class and as he did, he noticed the time. It was already after eleven and perhaps too late to just rock up to her home, but he could drive past and see if the lights were on. Decker made the drive in silence, enjoying the quiet and the handling of the car. He pulled onto the street where Savannah lived, thankful that Eidolon had the perk of being able to find information, both inane and life-changing, so easily. Her address hadn't been hard to find at all and the thought made him frown.

He slowed, seeing the numbers of the houses slip by until he got to number twenty-five and frowned. He'd maybe expected to see lights on but not to see Savannah in jeans and sweater scrubbing paint from her door. He was out of the car in a second and walking up the path. Her eyes widened when she saw him, a flicker of plea- sure before it was replaced by a wall of suspicion and indifference, which he deserved.

"What the hell happened?" He saw smudges of red paint and then his eyes made out the word beneath and his gut twisted, and tension made him straighten. Someone had written the word 'mur- derer' across her door and the thought made him furious that she'd be attacked in this way.

Savannah crossed her arms, the wet rag hanging from her hand as she glanced back at the door. "It's nothing, just a bit of graffiti."

Decker stepped around her body to get a better look and was struck by the reaction the person who'd written it had wanted. They'd wanted her to be afraid, to send a message, to intimidate.

"That isn't nothing, Savannah." His fists clenched and he had the desire to hit someone, preferably the someone who'd done this. He pulled his gaze away from the door and looked back at the woman who was calm in the face of it all and noticed the tiredness in her hazel eyes, which looked browner now, but he knew in the daylight they'd be an almost moss green with just flecks of gold at the edges.

"What do you want, Decker?" He could hear the fight and the strength that made her so alluring underneath the fatigue of the day and hated that he'd contributed to it in any way.

"I came to apologise for my behaviour. I was out of line and I'm sorry."

Savannah sighed and it was deep. Despite that, she nodded and smiled but it didn't reach her eyes. No, this was a polite smile reserved for public appearances, not the real kind that lit up a room. He hated it immediately, but he nodded in return. He had no right to demand more from her and he didn't want it anyway.

"Fine, apology accepted. Now, you can go. I have to get this finished before I go to bed, and it's been a long day."

"Let me help you, Savannah." He held out his hand for the cloth and she squinted, obviously not trusting him and she had every right.

"Why?"

Decker chuckled and shrugged. "Because we're friends and I want to help you."

Her head tilted as if she couldn't figure him out and right now, he couldn't either, but he knew he couldn't walk away and leave her to deal with this alone and not just because Astrid and Adeline would kill him. "We're not friends, Decker."

"Fine, then how about as a way to prove how sorry I am for being a jerk earlier?"

"Fine, whatever you need." Savannah turned back to the hot soapy water and dunked the rag before resuming her chore in silence. Decker slipped his jacket off and folded his shirt sleeves to the elbows before taking the rag from her hand and gently nudging her out of the way with his hip. She looked at him as if he were a bug under a microscope she couldn't figure out, and it was unsettling and yet he knew he wanted to be there to help her anyway.

"I'll get a scrubbing brush."

She walked away, coming back moments later with the brush and they worked side by side cleaning the mess made from the paint. It was comfortable with neither of them feeling the need to fill the silence. Instead, it felt right.

"Any idea who did this?"

He saw her shake her head out of his peripheral vision. "Nope, not a clue but my guess would be a disgruntled patient or relative. What I do isn't without risk and not every outcome is the one I hope for. You try to manage expectations but with brain surgery, and spinal too, there are no guarantees and people don't always fully accept that."

"Is there anyone in particular who might've done this?"

"I can't think of anyone off the top of my head."

Decker wiped the last of the pink suds away and the door was restored to its original condition. He was glad it was PVC, as a wooden door would've been impossible without a new paint job.

"Do you have security?"

"I have that." Savannah pointed up at a fake security alarm system that wouldn't deter anybody.

Decker scowled.

"That is not worth the twenty quid you paid for it. You need a security system put in. I'll sort it tomorrow."

Savannah crossed her arms over her chest, and he tried not to notice the curve of her breasts, or the way her eyes lit with fire making him want to kiss the lips that were pursed in anger again. Now he knew she tasted as sweet as she looked but more than that, she had a leashed passion inside her that he wanted to explore but he knew he'd blown any chance with her. Not that he wanted one, or did he?

The truth was he did, but she'd want more of him than he could give. Everything about her screamed commitment. Her job, the skill it took to do what she did was phenomenal, and her interactions with people showed she really cared. He had the worrying feeling that being with her would open him up to things he just wasn't prepared to deal with.

"No, I can handle this on my own. I don't need you swooping in here to soothe some misplaced guilt. You kissed me, you regretted it, and then felt bad for being a knob about it." Savannah leaned forward slightly, and he caught the scent of her perfume from earlier. "News flash, Decker, you're not the first man to reject me or be a dick. I absolve you of your guilt. Go about your life and I'll go about mine and we don't need to ever meet again."

He found himself unreasonably put out by her dismissal, and the thought of any man not wanting her gave him mixed feelings he couldn't understand. Gratitude because he felt suddenly relieved that she didn't have a man in her life but equally angry that anyone would think she wasn't the amazing, sexy, wonderful woman she was. That was until he remembered he was one of those men.

He was different and had his own reasons for not wanting to take this further. He was protecting her. A little voice told him he was protecting himself, but he shut it down. He stepped closer until his body was almost touching hers, her eyes locking on his, not backing down even a bit and he felt his dick twitch with desire. She'd be a firecracker in bed, all passion and heat.

"This isn't guilt, Savannah, this is me being a friend."

"I have enough friends. I don't need one who blows hot and cold."

Decker gritted his jaw, wondering if his teeth would survive being friends with her anyway.

"Fine, then let me do it because it would make Adeline and Astrid happy."

Savannah blinked and he could see the different thoughts moving over her expressive face as she considered his words.

"Fine. Price it up but I'm paying for it, and I don't want any bull-shit arguments either."

"You know, Dr Sankey, you have quite the mouth on you."

"You know, Mr Decker, I don't give a fuck."

She'd said it to shock him. She was usually the epitome of profes-sional and polite, and seeing her relaxed and off the clock, he found he liked her even more and that was dangerous. He didn't want to want her, but he did. Usually, he could walk away without looking back but for some reason, this woman was getting under his skin, and he had to shut it down and fast.

"So, I see. Well, I'll bid you goodnight, Dr Sankey."

He saw her lips twitch as if she'd won a point in a game he didn't know the rules to.

"Good night, Decker. Thank you for the apology and the help."

He inclined his head and walked away, slipping into his car and he waited until she closed the door and the lights turned off before he drove away.

She was far too beautiful and much too spirited, nothing like Susie had been. His wife had been sweet and gentle, a home maker who'd always deferred to him, even when he urged her to find her own voice and to tell him what she wanted but he'd loved her and she'd loved him, and he still missed the way her body would curl into him when he got into bed. Sex had been good, if a little rehearsed, but that wasn't the be-all and end-all in life and having Milo had been hard on her.

Maybe it was a good thing Savannah was so different from Susie. It would help him stay away from the very different Savannah Sankey or maybe that was the problem. The good doctor, and he knew she was excellent at what she did, was everything he didn't deserve. He didn't deserve to be happy and find love again and it was a risk he wasn't prepared to take, not for anyone—no matter how beautiful they were.

Either way, their paths shouldn't cross again. She was a temptation, and he never quite knew how he'd react to her and that was its own problem. Decker drove home to his silent house and parked the car in the garage before setting the alarm. It unsettled him to know Adeline's friend was alone with no security and some crazy person was hell-bent on making her life difficult.

Sleep wasn't easy that night. Dreams of Susie and Milo trapped in the car after the stricken truck driver had run the red light haunted him, before Susie morphed into Savannah Sankey, red blood dripping from her hands as she looked at him with accusation.

Around five am, he gave up and got up. He changed and went for a run, hoping the exercise would extinguish the nightmares. His legs and lungs were burning by the time he made it home and he still couldn't get the thought out of his head that something terrible had happened and that he should never have left her alone last night.

By nine am, he pulled on his leathers and took his bike out on the road, his mind taking him to the street where he'd been just last night. He stopped at the end of the road feeling like a stalker as he watched the still house, wondering if he should knock and check on her but not wanting to act like the stalker he suspected she might have.

At nine-thirty she stepped out onto her front porch in running gear and he watched, mesmerised as she did some stretches, the bra top and shorts hiding none of her considerable assets. He swallowed and willed away the desire that flooded him, his tongue thick in his mouth, his breathing fast, and he pulled his visor down before turning the bike around and driving away. She was fine and he'd sort the alarm out for her at cost and then he'd walk away.

Chapter Three

"And how is our patient feeling today?" Savannah looked down at her notes and then back up at nineteen-year-old Melissa Evans who'd been diagnosed with congenital scoliosis. Savannah had operated when the spinal cord had become impinged. That was two weeks ago and Missy, as she'd asked to be called, was doing well.

"Much better. Do you think I can go home soon?"

Savannah had the same conversation with her every day, but she had better news this time. "I think if the physio team is happy with your progress, we can look at getting you home by the weekend. How does that sound?"

"Amazing!" Missy squealed and it was hard not to return the infectious joy from a young woman who'd been through years of surgeries and pain and was coming out the other side. It was why she loved her job so much.

"Wonderful. I'll see you tomorrow and we'll get some images and go from there. Is mum coming in later?"

Missy nodded. "Yes, she had to go help my little brother get packed for a school trip, but she'll be here later."

Siobhan Evans was a single mum who'd worked her ass off for her kids and was devoted to them. Savannah liked her and respected all she'd done, that was the real hard work. Her part was done in weeks, but Siobhan had stress day in and day out.

Savannah finished up her ward rounds quickly and headed back to her office. She passed her ex-husbands office, glad that his door was closed. She didn't have the energy for his bullshit today. She could've left and gone to work elsewhere after the divorce, but she loved it there and why should she leave when she hadn't done anything wrong. The weekly meetings were a price she was prepared to pay for the job of her dreams.

She was nose deep in the case notes for a surgery she had coming up involving a particularly difficult tumour when there was a knock on her door and Andy poked his head in. Savannah fought the groan and pasted a look of indifference on her face. "What can I do for you, Andy?"

"I could do with a consult on a patient of mine if you have five minutes?"

Damn man knew she'd never turn down a patient and was using that excuse more and more of late to spend time with her. She needed to nip it in the bud before it became a thing. "Can Dr Rosco do it? I'm up to my eyes in patient notes."

Andy shook his head as he put his hands in his pockets and rocked back on his heels, watching her. Andy Farr was tall, slim, had a head of dark hair, brown eyes, and a crooked smile that seemed to melt the pants off women. She'd fallen victim to that and his silver tongue, which had promised so much and delivered so little.

For her though, it hadn't been his looks or the charm, it was the fact he was a brilliant surgeon. She could listen to him for hours when he talked shop with her, but his philandering had become the reason his name was mentioned more and more of late, and she pitied him for throwing it all away. She also suspected he was drinking pretty heavily but had never had proof. If she had, she would've reported him, a drunk neurosurgeon was a recipe for disaster.

"Rosco is in surgery."

Savannah fought the sigh and nodded, her lips pursed trying to contain her frustration. "Fine, what is it?"

Andy sat down in the chair opposite and proceeded to give her the details on the patient, he was halfway through when she realised it was an excuse, he'd done this particular surgery a thousand times and told him so.

He gave her a sheepish grin that had once worked wonders on her mood and felt nothing but irritation. "I miss you, Savannah."

Savannah breathed in through her nose. "No, you don't. You miss being married and the stability it gives you. You never loved me, Andy, and we both know it."

She stood hoping it would encourage him to leave, but he just gave her a hang dog expression.

"How can you say that? You're the only woman I've ever loved."

"Well, you had a funny way of showing it."

"I've changed, Savi. I'm not that man anymore."

"You are or you wouldn't be here saying this to me while your pregnant girlfriend is working three floors away." She had no love for this man anymore, he'd hurt her too badly, but she didn't hate him either and that was sadder than anything. She felt nothing but pity. "Andy, you're a brilliant surgeon, concentrate on that and the child you'll have very soon."

His eyes softened as he looked at her and they glistened with tears. "It should have been us, Savi. That child should have been ours."

A gut-punch of pain slammed into her at his words, and she clenched her fists to ward off the grief of what could've been. "But it isn't and never will be. I don't love you anymore, Andy. Go be a good father to your child and leave me in peace." She stepped towards the door and opened it, wanting this over so she could get on with her day.

Andy moved to the door and stopped inches from her as he passed, his eyes moving over her as if he didn't understand what had happened. "What happened to you, Savannah? You used to be so sweet and forgiving."

Savannah shrugged. "I grew up and realised that it was only worth showing my sweet side to those who deserved it and didn't use it to hurt me."

Andy's jaw tensed and his eyes grew cold in a look she'd seen before when he didn't get his own way. "You'll regret this."

"I doubt that. Now I have work to do." She waited, hoping she wouldn't have to have a slanging match with him.

"Fine, have it your way."

Savannah let out a long breath when he left and closed the door behind her, leaning on it slightly as her legs gave out a little. She was a strong, independent woman who'd excelled in her career beyond her hopes and dreams, but she'd never liked confrontations and still didn't, and that was the second time in three days she'd had to deal with an arrogant male.

Granted she didn't know Mark Decker well and shouldn't have been as wounded by his behaviour as she'd been. He'd made it clear he didn't like her, and she'd pushed it because she liked him. No, she didn't know him well enough to like him, but she was intrigued and definitely attracted to him.

He had a dark knight vibe going on, was surly and sexy with a past that screamed of pain. Yet he was protective of those he cared about and laughed freely with his friends. Then he'd gone and kissed her, and it had been the kind of kiss that changed lives or made the heavens open and angels rain down. She laughed at her own whimsy, but it had been the best kiss of her life and he'd gone and been a dick.

As she'd told Andy, she was sweet, but she was no longer a puppy to be kicked because some cruel kid got off on it and she wouldn't be that for him or the sexy as sin Mark Decker. She'd been right to forgive him, especially when he'd helped her clean her door like he had but she wouldn't lower her guard again. Once bitten twice shy was her new motto.

A knock on the door behind her had her sighing and turning to open it, ready to give Andy hell for being a pain in her ass. "What now?"

Her mouth dropped into a surprised O at the sight of Mark Decker looking devastatingly handsome in his three-piece suit, his dark hair styled perfectly and a look of surprise in his raised eyebrows.

"Is now a bad time?"

Feeling flustered, Savannah waved him inside her office and took the few seconds to close the door and walk to her seat to calm her shock at seeing him there. "Is Addie okay?" Her first thought was that her friend was in trouble or had somehow relapsed from her injuries of last year.

Decker held up a hand to stop her panic. "No, she's fine, but I wanted to bring the details of the new security system over for you to look at."

Savannah sat back in her chair trying to remain calmer than she felt. "Why? Lopez emailed me everything yesterday."

"Oh, I didn't realise that."

He was lying, she knew there was nothing that went on at Eidolon that this man didn't know about. He was too controlled not to have his finger on the pulse of every single thing. *Interesting*, but she didn't call him on it.

"Yes, he said he'd have Liam install it this week for me."

"I can get it done today if you like?"

They were taking this way more seriously than was needed but she'd go along with it for Adeline's sake. Her friend worried and she cared too much to put her through any more stress, plus an alarm wasn't a bad idea. "Sure, if you want but don't put yourself to any trouble."

"It's no trouble."

"Why are you really here, Mark?"

She thought she saw his shoulders stiffen but couldn't be sure before he locked his expression down and looked away to the window that overlooked the gardens of the private clinic. "I don't know."

She was surprised by his answer. Admitting he didn't know something wouldn't be easy for a man like him who kept everything so buttoned up. Yet, the more she saw him the more attractive she found him. He had a sense of purpose and stillness that seemed to pulse with energy. A danger that made her insides quake but not in fear, rather with hot, damning lust. No man had ever affected her this way, making her hot and needy with just a kiss or the memory of one and yet she didn't really like him all that much. He'd done more to make her wary of him than the opposite.

She felt bold in the face of his uncertainty. Leaning back on her chair she crossed her legs, thanking God she'd changed from her beloved crocs into black court shoes that made her legs look good. It was vain but she didn't care, she needed the confidence boost.

"Do you want to know what I think?" She waited until his unwavering gaze turned to her, his head cocked to the side and his eyes dancing devilishly.

"Oh, what do you think, Dr Sankey?" His lips twitched at the corner almost in a challenge for her to continue.

"I think you like me. Not like as in you want to be friends, but more that you want me in your bed."

His fingers steepled across his chest and she could see she'd surprised him, and the thought made her brazen. "Is that so?"

"Tell me I'm wrong."

He waited a beat, which felt like a year, and she wondered what had possessed her to play this game with him.

"You're not wrong and therein lies the problem. I don't want to want you. I don't want to wake up imagining your hands and mouth on my cock. I don't want to think about how your hot wet pussy might feel around my dick and yet I do."

Jesus Christ on a cracker? His words were like tiny explosives detonating a flood of desire in her body. Dirty talk had never done it for her before but it sure as hell did it now. She was all set to rip his damn clothes off and go at it on the desk, but she couldn't find her voice.

"Stuck for words suddenly, doc?" He stood and walked slowly around the desk until he was standing in front of her and bent his head until it was so close, she could smell the mint on his breath. Her heart began to hammer so hard she worried she might have a heart attack; butterflies of need and nerves flew around her belly. His lips against her ear were feather-light and she closed her eyes.

"Not going to happen, no matter how much I want you. You, Dr Sankey, are trouble with a capital T."

With that, he pulled away and she rocked forward. A deep chuckle moved through him as he backed toward the door. He had angled away but not enough that she couldn't see how much she affected him and damn, but it saved her from the humiliation of showing him her hand.

"May I remind you, Mr Decker, that you sought me out not the other way around. Perhaps you should try convincing yourself it won't happen because I'm sure I can stay away. Are you?"

His brow raised at her blatant challenge, and he took it like she'd known he would. "I never lose, Dr Sankey."

"Me neither."

He seemed to thrive on the competition, and she wondered if this game would come to anything as they never really had to see each other so keeping their hands to themselves should be easy enough.

"I'll collect your keys later and fit the alarm tomorrow."

Perhaps he was more up for this game than she thought. "Okay."

He winked and she fought her reaction to it as he closed the door. Her day had become infinitely better and stayed that way for the rest of the day.

Chapter Four

His jaw cracked as he yawned wide, and Decker groaned with joy as the first hit of caffeine hit his system. He'd slept for shit last night, all thanks to Dr Sankey. He frowned remembering the challenge in her gorgeous nut-brown eyes and the wide sexy smile that made his dick harden even now as he imagined those cherry-pink lips on him. She was trouble and yet she was sweet and clever, dedicated to her job and patients, and that made her so much more dangerous.

She wasn't the type of woman you fucked and walked away from, she was the ever after kind and exactly what he avoided like it was the plague. Yet for some inexplicable reason, he couldn't seem to stay away from her and that was the crux of the problem. He'd been telling the absolute truth when he'd said he had no idea why he'd sought her out yesterday, just that it had been something he couldn't stop.

Downing the last of his coffee, he took a quick shower and, instead of dressing in his usual suit and tie, he dressed in jeans and a t-shirt of dark burgundy that one of the girls, Callie he thought, had bought him for Christmas. Apparently, it brought out the warmth of his naturally tan skin. Realising he was dressing for her he took it off and put on a plain white one instead.

He may have challenged her to break first and fall under his spell, but he had no intention of getting caught in his own web. It was complex enough already.

She was Adeline's friend and she and Lopez were like family to him, the whole group were. Then there was the fact that being in a room with her and smelling her scent and watching the curve of her neck or the way she gathered her hair back from her face and draped it over one shoulder shouldn't be sexy—but it was.

He was aware enough to know he wanted her with a desperation that left his gut clenched and his cock hard as stone, but he couldn't fuck her and walk away. She'd take a part of him he wasn't prepared to give her.

Grabbing his jacket, he noticed it was still ridiculously early, only six-thirty and a devilish idea came to mind. He wondered what the sexy doctor looked like rumpled from sleep and if she'd mind if he woke her up. Deciding to find out, he left the house taking his truck and the equipment he'd need to add the alarm.

Despite all their playful banter, he knew she was a good person and hated the idea of her being so vulnerable. He'd like to get his hands on the asshole that thought it was okay to scare and intimidate her. His hands clenched on the steering wheel at the thought, and he had to physically relax his reaction to her in danger.

His truck cruised the quiet streets of the town he called home, only a few people were on the roads, and he sighed at the peace here. Hereford was surrounded by greenery and had a slower pace but still gave him enough of the culture and speed he needed from his days in New York. He sometimes felt like it had happened to another person, like he was a spectator to it all, and then he'd have a memory of his wife or son, and it would slam into his gut, taking his breath away with the pain.

Pulling up outside Savannah's home, he saw her car in the drive and smiled. He'd expected a prim little electric car but had been pleasantly surprised when he'd discovered she drove a sporty two-seater Audi—it suited her.

Grabbing his tools, he knocked on her door and waited. The house was silent and for a second, he wondered if maybe she was out, which led him to wonder where she was and if maybe she was with a man. An explosion of jealousy went off in his veins like napalm and he had to swallow past the growl that moved up his throat like some caveman. An intense hostility toward the nameless, faceless man made him clench his teeth.

The door opened and he looked down, his feeling moving from jealousy to lust in one beat of his heart. Savannah was staring up at him through bleary, slumberous eyes. Her hair was sticking up in wild disarray and she was wearing Garfield shorty pyjamas that looked like they'd seen better days and she was the sexiest fucking thing he'd seen in years.

"Mark, what are you doing here so early?"

His chest tightened at his name on her lips, the unfamiliar ache of desire pulling him closer. He wanted to taste her more than he wanted to breathe right now, to push her against the door and see if she was sweet as he imagined, if she was as soft and wet for him. He did none of those things. Instead, he frowned and pushed past her into her home, his eyes travelling over the small open plan space that was both homey and clutter-free.

"Mark!"

He turned then and saw her standing with her hands on her hips, her nipples poking through the thin cotton of her PJs.

"I'm here to fix the alarm." He stepped closer as if pulled by an invisible force. His fingers itched to touch her, and he held tight to his tool bag to stop himself, not because of the bet they'd made but because he was seriously struggling not to grab her and go at her like a neanderthal.

"At six-forty-five in the morning?" Her eyes went wide, and she raised her brow in a perfect arch, which was both haughty and cute.

"I'm a busy man and I have other things to do besides this."

Her face fell and he instantly hated himself for making her look contrite. God, why did she bring out his inner asshole?

"No, you're right, let me take a quick shower and get dressed and then I'll help you. That way you can be done quicker."

"Don't you have to work?"

Savannah shook her head and smothered a yawn, and he noticed the dark circles under her eyes.

She shook her head. "No, I was on call last night and had two surgeries back-to-back, so I'm off for two days."

"Shit. Sorry, I had no idea."

Savannah waved her hand away. "It's fine. Help yourself to coffee and I'll be down in a jiffy."

Decker watched her walk away and felt like a dick for waking her now. The job she did saved lives all the time and when she didn't save them, she made them better. He wasn't stupid, he knew from bitter experience that it didn't always go her way, but she most likely saved more than she didn't.

He found the coffee and put it on while he unloaded the rest of his kit. He didn't usually fit the alarms, but he'd helped the guys before and had done his own. He knew it hadn't gone unnoticed by Liam or Lopez that he'd taken over here and hoped they wouldn't give him a hard time over it.

It meant nothing, just that he had the time and was doing a favour for a friend of a friend. He snorted as he poured himself a cup of the rich smooth nectar and inhaled another sniff. He had very few vices these days, instead choosing to eat clean, not indulge in alcohol to excess, and feed his body and mind what it needed to be healthy. But coffee and the odd whiskey were his two vices, and he wasn't prepared to give those up. Not now or ever.

"Hey."

Savannah moved next to him, her hair still wet from the shower she'd taken, and his mind immediately imagined her naked and wet, the water gliding over her silky skin. His body got tight, and he had to force himself to step away in case he reached for her. He'd been so engrossed in his thoughts she'd snuck up on him and that hadn't happened to him in longer than he could remember. She was wearing skinny jeans and an old University College London hoodie. He knew she'd done her neuro training down there, but he realised he didn't know much else, apart from that she was divorced.

He snorted as he saw her pour coffee into a mug which read 'Yes, I'm a doctor. No, I don't want to look at it!'

"So, what can I do to help?"

"Honestly, not a lot."

"Mark, if you don't put me to work, I'm going to crash and then you'll have to put up with me snoring on the sofa."

His lips twitched in a rare smile, and he found himself not just lusting after her but liking her more with every interaction. "Okay, doc, let's get you a job to do."

Her smile was genuine, and for the rest of the morning they worked side by side, with her handing him tools and asking him questions about mundane things. Normally preferring quiet, he found her mellow tones soothing and easy.

Around lunchtime he noticed she was flagging, her conversation slowing, and when he looked around, she was fast asleep in the armchair, almost sitting upright. He felt bad again for waking her.

Placing the cable he was using aside, he moved closer to her and crouched, balancing on the balls of his feet as he did. She looked nothing like the siren who'd challenged him yesterday. She'd been sexy as all hell, but this Savannah tugged at his heart in much more dangerous ways. She made him want things, like to kiss her, and protect her, to wake up with her. She was funny and clever, sexy and caring and it was a deadly combination.

"I don't want to want you."

He rubbed a lock of her hair between his fingers and wondered what it would feel like gliding over his chest. A pang of regret moved through him, what it could be like if he was a different man. If he wasn't battling the guilt and the demons he tried to keep locked up so damned tight all the time. What-ifs swam through his head as he bent and lifted her into his arms with infinite tenderness, that he'd deny and brush off as something anyone would do.

He settled her against him and walked to her stairs as she snuggled closer against his body and sighed in contentment, his movements not waking her.

She must be exhausted.

He found her room, the scent of her filling it and making his jeans feel tight in the crotch. Pulling back the quilt, he laid her down. She rolled onto her side, her hands going beneath her cheek like an innocent child.

Bending, he pulled off her boots, taking care not to wake her, and pulled the quilt around her. Stepping back, he wondered at the urge to climb in next to her and pull her into his arms. To hold her as she slept and listen to the sounds of her breathing, her warmth surrounding him.

It had been so long since he'd held a woman while she slept. His wife had been the last person he'd touched that way. He wasn't a monk and he'd fucked around plenty but holding them while they slept, falling asleep with a woman, was something he didn't allow himself. It came with too much risk. Yet as he watched Savannah sleep, he found himself wanting that more and more. He didn't know what it was about the good doctor, but she'd woken something in him, and he was having a hard time shoving it back in the box marked 'do not open'.

It was the reason he'd dismissed her at the wedding, why he felt the desire to needle her every chance he got. Because deep down he knew she had a power over him that if he allowed her in, she'd break down his carefully constructed walls and leave what was left of his heart exposed, and he couldn't take that chance.

He wondered if there was a way to have both. Have her in his life and in his bed, and still keep his heart safe and tucked away, where nobody could cause him the kind of pain that still left him having panic attacks in the middle of the night.

Rules, that was what he needed. Maybe if they had rules, they could play out this crush, get rid of this lust and stay safe. Just like the suits he wore were his armour against people approaching, and his aloof attitude stopped people from getting close unless he deemed them safe. Maybe a strict set of rules would allow him to have his cake and eat it.

Looking at her sleeping, he very much wanted to eat his cake.

Chapter Five

Savannah frowned at the insistent sound of buzzing from beside her and forced her eyes open enough to grab for her phone. She blinked, confused about where she was and how. The last thing she remembered was helping Mark. Grabbing her phone, she noticed it was still light but that the sky was hazy with the glow of the late afternoon sun.

Checking her phone, she saw a text from a number she didn't know, and her belly dropped wondering if it was more games from her ex-husband.

Sitting up she pushed her hair from her face and opened the text.

UNKNOWN: WAKEY, WAKEY, SLEEPY HEAD. I FINISHED THE ALARM AND LOCKED UP WHEN I LEFT. DO YOU HAVE TIME LATER TO MEET ME FOR A DRINK? I HAVE A PROPOSITION FOR YOU.

Savannah put down the phone and looked out her window realising the house was still and quiet. Reading the message again she found herself intrigued, her heart rate picking up in anticipation of what he might suggest. He'd probably ask her to leave the country and never come back and never darken his door again. Apart from fitting the alarm and that one incendiary kiss, he'd never shown her for one second that he liked her, and it bugged the hell out of her.

Oh, he might want to shag her brains out but hate sex was a real thing and that was very different. That was chemicals and hormones, she knew all about that. When she looked at Mark Decker though, she saw, or had seen, more than his dashing good looks and the confidence that he showed the world. She saw a man who hid his pain behind iron control, and she wondered if it was her nature to fix things. Her shoulders rose and fell in a sigh of confusion as she re-read the message. Adding his name into her phone under 'Sexy Asshole', she smiled and decided to take a leap of faith and find out what he wanted from her.

As she swung her legs out of bed to go and relieve her bladder, she wondered how she'd got to bed and who had taken her boots off. Had Mark carried her up here and removed her boots while she slept? It felt so intimate that he'd seen her in a vulnerable state and shown her kindness. Was there more to him than his devilish good looks and his snark or was she seeing something that wasn't there?

Washing and drying her hands, she picked up her phone from the counter in her bathroom as it buzzed. She looked down at it as she made her way into the kitchen in search of food, her belly rumbling as if to remind her she hadn't eaten.

SEXY ASSHOLE: THE ALARM CODE IS BY THE COFFEE WITH INSTRUCTIONS. AND I HAVEN'T MISSED THAT YOU READ MY MESSAGE AND IGNORED MY INVITATION! CHICKEN?

Savannah scowled at her phone and began to reply. She didn't owe him a response and knew this was a trick to get his way, but she was curious enough to respond anyway, and he'd done her a massive favour with the alarm, and she felt like she owed him.

SAVANNAH: I WAS DECIDING IF I WAS CURIOUS ENOUGH TO FIND OUT!!!!

SEXY ASSHOLE: AND???

SAVANNAH: FINE. WHERE AND WHEN?

SEXY ASSHOLE: SIX PM IN THE ROSE AND CROWN.

Savannah: Fine. See you there.

He didn't reply but she could see it had been read. After shovelling a tuna mayo and cheddar cheese sandwich down her throat, she went up to shower and change. She didn't want to make too much effort but enough to make him regret being such a dickhead and rejecting her. This wasn't about trying to attract him, it was now about saving face and making him see what he was missing without being overt.

She wished she could call Addie and talk to her but with Mark being her friend it didn't feel right. Maybe she'd try and get some advice from her tomorrow. They'd planned to meet up for lunch in town and do some shopping so it would be the perfect opportunity.

In the end, she decided on a pair of soft jeans with rips in the thigh and a dusky pink oversized top that hung off her shoulder. Adding some small gold hoops and a bangle, she touched her eyelashes with mascara and put some clear gloss on her lips. She left her hair in waves that fell to her shoulders. Sitting back, she assessed her look and grabbed her bag before she could second guess herself.

The Rose and Crown was fairly busy when she arrived, and she glanced around the bar for Mark before finding him sitting in a corner booth. He lifted his head as she walked over and nodded, giving nothing away as to why he'd asked her to meet him.

She slid into the booth opposite him and placed her bag beside her. "Hey, sorry I'm late. I couldn't find a parking spot."

He lifted a glass of what looked like soda to his lips and took a sip as she tried hard to look away from the masculine column of his throat as he swallowed. She'd thought he'd be back in his suit, but he'd surprised her wearing a different pair of jeans and a navy shirt, and a brown leather jacket lay across the back of his chair. He looked good, his dark eyes sparkling and warm, but then he always looked good.

"That's okay, I only just got here. Can I get you a drink?"

"Uh, yeah sure. Just an apple juice please."

"Sure, I'll be right back."

He stood and she caught the scent of his cologne; it was musky and heady and made her senses swim. Taking a deep breath, she tried to get her heart rate under control as he came back and handed her the apple juice. Savannah took it gratefully and thanked him, taking a sip, and placing it on a coaster with the local brewery name on it.

"So, what is this all about?"

"Well, I think it's clear we find each other attractive." Savannah snorted and Mark looked up sharply. "Am I wrong?"

She shook her head and took another drink, wishing it was wine but knowing with being on call almost always meant it was a bad idea.

"No, you're not wrong, at least from my side. But you know this already, Mark, and you made it very clear you're not interested in anything with me. That's fine, I get it. Let's just agree to be civil for our friends' sakes."

Mark was shaking his head. "No."

"No?" Savannah wasn't sure if it was fatigue still catching up with her or if this conversation really made no sense.

"No, I'm interested, just not in a relationship. You want love and forever and I can't give you that, but I can give you fun and enough orgasms to make it worth your time."

Savannah felt her mouth drop open and then close as his words rebounded in her brain. Orgasms from Mark Decker sounded phenomenal. She clenched her legs together under the table as desire pooled in her belly and her clit throbbed. "Orgasms?"

Mark leaned in closer, and she could feel his minty breath on her neck. His deep voice as he spoke the next words reminding her of the kiss they'd shared, the one she'd tried and failed to forget. "So many orgasms you won't be able to get out of bed."

Savannah couldn't deny she liked the sound of that but her previous encounters with this man had made her wary. "Why the change of heart?"

Mark shrugged his powerful shoulders. "I want you and you want me."

"But no feelings?" Savannah needed to be sure she had this right before she made a decision.

"No. Absolutely no feelings and no sleepovers or promises. This is just sexy and fun, nothing more. Outside of the bedroom, we're strictly friends only."

"Are we friends, Mark?"

He took another sip of his drink as if stalling. "I know we got off to a rough start, and I take full responsibility for that. I was fighting my attraction to you, but now I have it all figured out."

Savannah was glad someone did because she wasn't entirely sure she did. She wanted Mark, of that there was zero doubt, but could she keep her heart safe from him? Casual sex wasn't her thing but if her track record was any indication neither were relationships. Her job took up so much of her energy and maybe not having to make promises of more would be good. She could have great sex and maybe a friend and no commitment. "So, friends with benefits essentially?"

"Yes, exactly."

"And if one of us meets someone or decides they want out we just shake hands and walk away without this affecting our friendship or hurting anyone?"

"Perfect."

"Okay, then I'm in."

Savannah stuck out her hand and Mark took it, his much larger palm enclosing hers, in a firm shake that had her wondering about what other talents his hands might have and how the slight calluses would feel on her soft skin.

Mark smiled and then brought her hand to his lips, making her shiver with need. She may have bitten off more than she could chew with this, but it was time to take a few risks. She did it every day with her job but until now had played it safe in her private life and what had that gotten her except an ex-husband with a big ego.

He released her hand slowly, his eyes intense and focused on her. "So, tell me more about your job. How did you decide to become a neurosurgeon?"

Savannah relaxed a little and answered his question. Mark, she found out, was easy to talk to, clever, funny, and attentive. He really listened with no pretence and not as if he was waiting for the attention to turn back to him.

"Have you ever been to Devon?" Savannah found herself asking after she explained how her parents had retired there.

"No, been to Cornwall on a job but I haven't actually been on a vacation since I started at Eidolon."

"No way. I know Jack is focused but surely he gives you time off?"

Mark chuckled and the sound moved through her like liquid honey. "Of course he does, but I hate taking time off. Vacations are for families and couples."

He sounded sombre for a split second before he seemed to snap out of it and pasted the fake smile back on his face. Although fake was wrong, it seemed genuine but as if only half his heart was involved, and the other half was locked away. It made her curious as to what pain was in his past but knew asking would be met by a stony-faced wall of silence.

"Well, if you ever get the chance or have the inclination, you should go. It's the most beautiful part of the world, full of quaint seaside villages and the beaches are as good as any you'd find in the Mediterranean."

"Maybe I will one day."

Savannah was about to respond when her phone, which was on the table, rang and she saw the hospital's name flash up. "Sorry. I have to get this."

"It's fine."

"Hello, Dr Sankey speaking."

Savannah locked eyes with Mark who gave her a small smile of understanding.

"Dr Sankey, it's Sadie Corner."

Savannah could hear the worry in the normally unshakeable woman's voice. "Oh hi, Sadie. What can I do for you?"

"I'm sorry to bother you but I didn't know who else to call."

"What's wrong?" Savannah sat up straighter, her hand moving to her bag and Mark seemed to go on high alert.

"It's Dr Farr. He's about to go into surgery and do bleed repair on a nineteen-year-old male who was the victim of a bar fight but he's...."

Sadie stopped and Savannah was already standing as Mark followed. "Go on?"

"He's drunk, Dr Sankey. I can smell it on his breath but when we challenged him, he got angry and threw me out of the operating theatre."

"I'm on my way. Try and stall him."

Sadie sighed in relief down the phone. "Okay, we'll try."

Savannah hung up and looked around for her car in a panic.

"Hey, what's going on?" Mark grabbed her arm to stop her forward momentum.

"One of the surgeons I work with is about to do surgery and apparently he's drunk. I have to go and stop him."

"Jesus fucking Christ." Mark looked calm but she could see he was angry by the way his jaw went tight. "Here, let me drive you. Your car is blocked in by that van."

She realised he was right, and some dickhead had blocked her car in, and she was trapped. "Okay, thank you."

Mark opened her car door and she got in as he moved around and jumped in the driver's seat.

"Do you know this person?"

Savannah snorted as she typed a text to her boss to meet her at the hospital and that it was urgent. She couldn't and wouldn't cover this up. Andy was putting innocents at risk now and his behaviour had to be dealt with. He was a good doctor but right now he was a liability and a danger to those around him.

"Yeah, you could say that." Mark gave her a sharp glance in question. "It's my ex-husband."

"Oh, I see."

Mark said no more but pushed the accelerator to the floor. At the hospital, he parked close and followed her inside like some body-guard not willing to leave her side. Savannah had no time to process it as Sadie met her walking down the hall and was in a state of panic.

"I'm sorry I couldn't stop him."

Savannah was pulling her jumper over her head and changing into scrubs as she moved toward the scrub room for theatre two. Inside she could see Andy at the head of the table as she shucked her jeans and pulled up her blue work uniform and shoved her feet in crocs. She scrubbed her hands as quickly as she could before she realised Mark was still beside her, but his eyes were on Andy, who was about to cut into the brain of a teenager while intoxicated.

She had to put her fury aside to concentrate on what she needed to do next, but a small part of her was glad Mark was there. He made her feel secure in a way she'd never know she needed before.

Chapter Six

The roar of blood was ringing in his ears; he was so angry he could hardly see straight. He felt movement beside him and watched as Savannah moved into the theatre, gowned and gloved and ready to take over from the dipshit asshole who was swaying on his feet with a scalpel poised in his hand. Mark's gut clenched with anxiety, and he walked toward the door, not wanting to leave Savannah alone with this man.

Her ex-husband of all people. He wanted to rush and grab the man by the throat and teach him a lesson he wouldn't soon forget but he knew the situation was precarious at best. One wrong move and that kid could lose his life.

Ignoring the hated stench of hospitals that brought back so many ugly memories, he watched through the glass, ready to step in if he was needed. Savannah looked calm and composed as if she dealt with this kind of thing every day.

"Andy!" She called the man's name in a soft voice, and he turned and glared at her.

"What do you want?"

He sounded antagonistic and defensive, and Mark's hands fisted at his side, and he took a step closer to the door.

"Andy, step away from that boy. You seem tired. Let me take over so you can go and rest."

"Oh, now you care. Now you want to listen to me." He was waving the scalpel around as the two nurses and the anaesthetist watched on, seemingly holding their breath.

"Andy, you know I care, and I'll listen, but you need to let me do this. You can't operate like this. Look at your patient and tell me you're giving him your very best."

Andy glanced at the boy and back to Savannah who'd moved closer, her hand outstretched to take the scalpel.

Suddenly Andy crashed the instruments by his side to the floor, the metal clanging together in the silent room as he grabbed for Savannah. Taking her by the arm, he pushed her against the wall as the nurses screamed and the other doctor put himself between them and the unconscious kid on the table who was thankfully unaware.

Mark felt his blood turn to ice as the glint of the blade against Savannah's perfect throat caught his eye. He moved slowly inside the theatre, knowing he shouldn't interfere but not able to stop himself. Savannah glanced at him and then back at Andy.

"Andy, don't do this. Let me go and we can talk after. I need to help this boy first."

"I need another chance, Savi. I need you to take me back. Let me back into your life."

Andy Farr was snivelling and crying like a broken man, but Mark didn't feel a single moment of sympathy. All he wanted to do right now was rip him apart. He planted his legs apart ready to move if he got the chance, his muscles almost quivering with rage.

"Okay, let me help this boy and then we'll talk."

"You promise?"

Mark saw Savannah swallow and the nerves and fear she was trying to hide as she talked her ex down. He was beginning to think there was way more to Savannah Sankey than he'd realised.

"Yes, I promise."

"Okay."

He dropped the blade and Mark moved, wrestling Andy off Savannah and shoving his face into the wall, pinning his arms behind his back.

"Get off me. Who the fuck are you?"

Andy wriggled to get Mark to let go but he only tightened his hold. "Your worst fucking nightmare, asshole." Mark pushed him harder against the wall, feeling a sense of satisfaction when the man cried out in pain. Served the fucker right for attacking Savannah and that was without allowing himself to think about the poor kid on the table whose brain he'd been about to hack into.

"Deck, do you have this? I need to operate on this boy."

"Yeah, I got it. Do your thing, doc."

Savannah gave him a brief nod and swung into action, giving orders, and taking control of the room. Mark wished he could stay and watch her in action, but he needed to get Andy, who was still whining, out of the room. Deck smiled when he saw Detective Aubrey Herbert waiting for them outside the operating room with two uniformed officers.

"I thought you told Will you were having a quiet night in and couldn't make poker night."

Aubrey was Will's fiancée. Mark personally thought his boss, a silent partner at Eidolon, should hurry up and marry the clever and beautiful detective and stop dicking around.

"What can I say, I got bored."

"Hmm." Aubrey flattened her lips and said no more although he knew she wanted to.

"This man assaulted me, and I want to press charges." Andy tried to jerk out of Decker's grip but got nowhere fast when Decker just tightened his hold.

Mark glared at Andy Farr as he handed him over to the two uniformed officers.

Aubrey raised a brow as she stepped forward. "Is that so? Well,

I'd think medical malpractice and threatening Dr Sankey's life is the bigger of your problems right now, Dr Farr."

Mark smirked at the red-faced man who looked pathetic now. He was tall and slim, and some would say good looking, but he was in no way good enough for Savannah. A beauty like her could have any man she wanted. She was clever, kind, funny, and could have her pick so why had she chosen Andy Farr?

Ha, she agreed to friends with benefits with you, asshole.

What had made her agree to it? He knew why he wanted it. She was everything he shouldn't want, and he couldn't stay away, and this allowed him the best of both worlds. But what was her reasoning? The thought made him oddly uncomfortable, and he pushed it away.

He watched as the two uniformed officers led Andy Farr away and the Medical Director came rushing toward them. The man was short, balding, with half-rimmed spectacles perched on his nose and a pinched look on his face, but when he got to them, he smiled and shoved his hand toward him.

"I'm Percy Gromadski, the Medical Director here. I can't thank you enough for your help."

Decker smiled at the man, getting a genuine feel about him. "Mark Decker, I'm a friend of Dr Sankey and was with her when the call came in, so it was no problem at all."

"Well, I thank you anyway. Andy Farr is a wonderful doctor. At least he was but he's been sailing down the wrong path these last few years, and this is the final straw. Dr Sankey, however, is one of our shining stars."

"I'm sure she is."

Deck could feel Aubrey watching him and knew she was taking in every single word especially the bit about him being with Savannah when the call came. Before he knew it, the entire team would be up in his business. Moving down the hall, he scrubbed his hands down his face. This was getting out of control already, but he couldn't seem to walk away.

An image of her at Jack and Astrid's wedding looking good

enough to eat popped into his mind and made his dick twitch with desire. He wasn't sure what it was about the good doctor, but she affected him in ways no other woman did. It was like some visceral need had pounded through him from the minute he'd met her.

The first time he'd seen her it had felt like a sucker punch, and he'd rejected it violently, acting like a complete wanker towards her, when what he really wanted was to pull her close and whisper all the things he wanted to do to her in her ear and feel her softness against his skin.

Getting to know her tonight was the most fun he'd had in a long time with a woman outside of the bedroom and it terrified him. Deciding he needed coffee, he went in search of the canteen and found it closed. He glanced at his watch and realised it was already eleven pm. He found a vending machine and bought himself a black coffee, wincing when he took his first sip and it tasted revolting. Dumping it in the trash, he bought a bottled water and wandered back toward the theatre where Aubrey was still waiting.

"Hey, you still here?"

"Yeah, I drove Savannah, so I thought I'd wait until she finishes to give her a lift home."

"I didn't know you two were a thing." Aubrey cocked her head as if the question wasn't loaded. The whole team knew he didn't date and some of the reason why, so this was new.

"We aren't. We're just friends."

"With benefits?"

Decker looked down at the far too intuitive woman and raised a brow.

She laughed and held her hands up. "Sorry, you know if I don't get the dirt my girls will kick my ass."

"You could, you know, not tell them?" he suggested, knowing he was pissing in the wind with that one.

"No way. This is far too juicy not to share."

"Well, I hate to disappoint but nothing has happened between us. It's strictly platonic." He didn't add that as soon as he could, he'd be changing that.

"Well, that sucks."

Decker laughed and took a seat, stretching out his legs. "You waiting to get a statement from Savannah?"

"Yeah, I need to know what happened. The nurses have given statements, but I still need to talk to the scrub nurses inside and the other doctor."

"It could be a while. I don't know what happened to that kid, but it sounded bad."

"I know, and now Savannah has to fix it. I'm not sure I could do it after what happened in there."

"Me neither."

What he wanted to do was tell Aubrey how amazing Savannah had been, how calm, how in control. Every sinew in his body had wanted to protect her, to rush in and save her and he'd fought the feeling hard because she wasn't his to protect but she'd saved herself and, perversely, it only made him want her more.

"Why don't you go, and I can let her know that she needs to come in tomorrow to give a statement?"

"Yeah, probably a good idea. I'll leave a message with Percy for the others. Talk soon, Deck."

"Yeah, goodnight, Aubrey."

He watched her walk away and settled in to wait for the doc to come out. He needed to see with his own eyes she was okay and maybe hold her in his arms. Not because he needed it but because she might. *Ha. Lying to yourself already? That didn't take long.* He pushed the thought away.

It was hours later, and the night was still, the hustle and bustle of the day long since silenced, when the door opened, and Savannah walked out, pulling the scrub cap off her head. She looked exhausted and pale, like she was dead on her feet. Decker rose and went toward her, wanting to ask how it went but afraid of the answer.

He was surprised when Savannah walked straight up to him, and face planted in his chest. His arms came up and around her and he did what he'd wanted to do earlier and held her. He could smell the vanilla and cherry scent of her shampoo mixed in with the chemical smells of the hospital, felt the warm weight of her as she leaned on him. It had been so long since he'd held a woman like this, and he found he needed it too. His hand smoothed the back of her ponytail and his fingers itched to wrap around it and pull her head back so he could kiss her and hear her sigh as he made his way down her neck with his lips.

"How's he doing?" He knew if he didn't distract himself, he'd follow through on what he was thinking. He pulled away but kept his hands on her arms to keep her steady and because he didn't want to stop touching her.

"If he makes it through the next twenty-four hours, he has a shot."

Savannah swayed and he gripped her elbow tight as he led her toward her office, which was on the same floor. He opened the door and pushed her gently toward the couch and sat beside her, pulling her into his chest and ignoring the persistent call that this was a bad idea.

"Sorry. I think it's all catching up with me."

Her hand was on his chest, her body curled into him, and he liked it and hated it at the same time. Fuck, if this was the way she affected him before he slept with her what the hell would it be like afterwards? No, not slept. Had sex because sleeping wasn't allowed.

"I'm not surprised. You were like a superhero in there."

Savannah lifted her head and smirked. "Are you kidding? I was terrified and so damn angry at Andy. No, I'll leave the superhero stuff to you guys at Eidolon. I'm gonna stay in my lane and just do my thing."

Decker dipped his head and his lips brushed hers and she gasped. He tilted her head up with his fingers under her chin and kissed her, savouring the feel of her, the taste that was all her and seemed to intoxicate him. She opened for him and met him with fervour and passion, but no aggression. The kiss was slow, languid, and conveyed what he couldn't give her in words. How much he wanted her, respected her, admired her.

She broke the kiss before he was ready. "Wow, if I could get that in a drip form, I'd never need to sedate a patient again."

Decker smiled. "Are you saying I'm like a drug?"

"Hell, yeah. It should be illegal."

"Well, that's the most perverse compliment I've ever had, but I'll take it."

Savannah fought a yawn, covering it with the back of her hand.

"For the record, doc, I think you're a superhero. You literally save lives every day and do things other people will never understand or be able to do. You handled that situation like a pro, and nobody would've known you were scared. I've seen trained operatives crumble under much less pressure."

"Ah, thanks. I guess I'm used to dealing with Andy, although tonight was different. He's never been that bad before."

"Hmm."

Decker couldn't say more, he was too angry and struggling to keep it under control. Every muscle in him wanted to find Andy Farr and teach him all the reasons why a woman like Savannah should never have to put up with the shit he'd been serving her. He didn't know the details but now he was going to make it his business to find out every single thing about the man and make him suffer. Savannah was a queen and deserved to be treated as such. He may not be her happily ever after and what they had, which was growing more complex by the day, might have an expiry date and rules but while she was in his bed, she'd be treated how she deserved.

"Let's get you home to bed."

He saw desire light her eyes and wanted to grin at her eagerness, but tonight wasn't the night. He wanted her fully energised and not ready to fall asleep standing up.

"I can't. I have to be on call in case he needs me. We're down a neurosurgeon with Andy gone until Percy can replace him."

He didn't like the idea of this being on her shoulders but what could he do? "Fine but you need to sleep. At least get some rest on the couch."

He pulled a blanket from the back of the couch and placed it over her as she lay down on her side and put her hands under her cheek like she had earlier that day. It felt like a lifetime ago already. So much had changed, not least his belief that he could walk away from her, but he would when this was over. When the time was right, he'd set her free.

"Will you stay with me?" Her voice was shy and unsure, still cautious of him after he'd been such an asshole to her.

"Yeah, I'll stay."

Tonight he'd stay and hold her because it felt like the most natural thing in the world to him. He tucked himself in behind her on the small couch and felt her wriggle to get comfortable. He cursed his damn reaction to her as he moved his hips back a little so his dick wouldn't be stabbing her in the back. Wrapping his arm around her waist, he felt his steely maintained walls begin to crumble and he had no clue how to fix them without hurting them both.

Chapter Seven

Savannah slipped out from beneath Mark's arm even though she wanted nothing more than to stay there. She had patients to check on and ward rounds to make. Using her private bathroom, she washed her face and brushed her teeth and tried to make herself look less like she felt, which was knackered.

She paused at the door, her hand on the handle as she looked at the man who'd taken care of her when she'd needed it. Mark Decker was such a contradiction, cold and unforgiving one minute with a tongue that could slice through a heart, and the next he was kind and gentle and everything she'd ever wanted.

Swallowing the sigh, she walked out, silently closing the door. They'd agreed to be friends with benefits, and she wanted that, but she was also afraid that the more she saw him, the more she'd want from him, and he'd made it clear he couldn't and wouldn't offer her more.

Pushing it from her brain, she checked on Corey Malcolm, the boy she'd operated on and found him awake. He was groggy but responding well and seemed to have full cognitive function, but a slight weakness on his left side. She ordered more tests and spoke with his devastated family, who were being looked after by Percy personally.

Once that was done, she realised she was starving and as it was already after eleven, she decided she'd get some brunch. She went to her office and found the couch empty and the blanket folded. She felt a pang that he was no longer there but had expected it. They were friends, not a couple. Why would he be there waiting like a sap for her to finish? He had a job of his own to do and had wasted enough time on her the last two days.

Shaking off the melancholy, she made her way to the canteen, loving the familiar sounds and energy of the place. She grabbed herself a green smoothie and a full English breakfast with bacon, sausage, scrambled eggs, mushrooms, and beans and sat down at the corner table. The rumour mill was working hard already and as she ate, she caught snippets of conversation about what had happened and spoke to a few people who stopped by her table.

One of those people was Ricky Grimes, a student doctor who was doing his rotation on the paediatric ward.

"Hey, Dr Sankey."

"Hi, Ricky. How are you?"

He sat down and nodded almost violently. "Good, good. I heard what happened with Dr Farr. Are you okay?"

"Yes, I'm fine, thank you."

She had no intention of getting involved in gossip with him. He had a little bit of a crush on her, and she was always careful not to encourage it with the junior doctors who she was training in any way. Being a woman in this job was hard, being a woman who slept with her co-workers was worse and she'd worked damn hard to shed that image after the disaster that was Andy Farr.

"I heard he hurt you."

Ricky sat up straighter as if he was trying to look all manly and alpha and she couldn't help but compare him to Mark and then felt bad. He was never going to measure up, at least in her head. "I'm perfectly fine as you can see, and I would remind you this could be a possible lawsuit for the hospital so perhaps refrain from gossip of any kind."

He blushed at the small reprimand and got up with a nod. "Yes, Dr Sankey."

She watched him rush off and sighed.

"Wow, I think you broke his heart!"

Savannah gasped in surprise when Mark sat down and tried to hide her pleasure at seeing him. "Mark, what are you doing here?"

He held his hand over his chest. "And the blows keep coming."

She dropped her eyes to her plate which was almost empty before pushing it aside and lifting her smoothie to her lips. "Sorry, I didn't mean it like that."

He pointed behind him with his thumb. "Who's the kid you just crushed?"

"One of the junior doctors."

"He has a massive crush on you."

"Yeah, I feared as much."

"So, apart from breaking hearts, how has your morning been?"

Mark was dressed once more in his three-piece suit, this one navy with a white shirt and a royal blue and white striped tie. He was back behind his metaphorical armour, although he didn't seem quite so tense today as he usually was.

"I did patient rounds and checked in with our patient from last night."

"How is he?"

"Awake and aware. He seems to have full capacity but some left-sided weakness. I've ordered more tests but overall, much better than I could've hoped."

"That good. And what about you? How are you doing?"

"Honestly, I'm okay. It might hit me later but at the moment it's just one more thing from my ex to deal with."

"I can't believe you were married to that guy."

Savannah snorted. "Me either."

"So, not sure if you've checked your phone but Aubrey has a big mouth and I've been fielding questions all morning from the team about us."

Savannah's eyes widened. "Really? All those big alpha males are gossiping?"

Mark laughed and it did funny things to her belly, making her heart beat faster and her brain wish for things she couldn't have. "Oh, they are the worst. They're like the worst sewing circle ever."

"So, what did you tell them?"

He glanced around the room before his dark, sultry gaze landed on her again. "That we're friends and that the rest is none of their business."

"Umm, wonder if that will work on Addie. I'm meant to be seeing her later but will need to cancel if Percy can't find someone to cover for me."

"Probably not. Women are much better at finding shit out than men."

"True, but it's the truth. We're friends and if we ever get a second of peace, we may be fuck buddies."

"Hey, don't call it that." He reached for her hand and twined his fingers through hers. "We may not be the next big love but don't denigrate it with those words."

"Fine, what would you call it?"

"Two adults who want to explore their mutual attraction without the constraints of expectation."

"Okay. It's a bit long-winded though, don't you think?"

Mark chuckled. "Maybe. So, are you busy tomorrow night?"

"I honestly don't know, but if we can get cover then I should be off."

"Great. How about we grab dinner at my place?"

Savannah felt her belly flutter with excitement and knew she needed to rein it in around him. It would be all too easy to fall for Mark when he was being sweet like he had been the last few days, but that wasn't all he was. He had another side that cut like a blade and that was the edge she should guard against.

"I can eat before I come over. No need to make this something it's not."

Mark stood abruptly and she got the feeling she'd angered him in some way and regretted it. He moved behind her and leaned over her chair, placing one hand on the table in front of her and the other on the back of her chair. He bent close and she could feel his warm, minty breath on her neck.

"Dinner at my place, seven pm. Don't be late. I'll text you the address."

Savannah shivered at his words that weren't a request but a command. From any other man, it was one that would have her bristling but from him it made her insides turn to jelly. Her breath came fast, and her heart slammed into her too-dry throat. She swallowed and nodded, not able to get the words out, but it seemed to be enough because she felt the brief brush of his lips against her hair and then he was striding for the exit.

She sat unmoving as she watched the perfect fit of his suit flex over strong shoulders as he strode with confidence toward the door as if he owned the room and everyone in it. He sure owned her body right this moment.

Taking a shaky breath and the last sip of her smoothie, she grasped hold of her equilibrium and stood. She still had work to do and cover to find because come what may, she'd be on his doorstep tomorrow night. Nothing would stop her from feeling all that tightly leashed control focused on her pleasure, and she knew without a shadow of a doubt that Mark Decker was a man who made sure a woman was satisfied in bed.

The rest of her day was an exercise in control as she battled patient care and heads of department meetings with Percy. The hospital had some serious damage control to do after last night.

She was at the boardroom table, seconds from banging her head in frustration when she got a text from Addie.

Addie: Can't do lunch, want to grab dinner tonight instead?

Hell, yes, she wanted to grab dinner with her friend and preferably a bottle of wine.

SAVANNAH: HELL YES, BE AT MINE AT SIX AND BRING WINE. I'LL ORDER TAKEOUT.

Addie responded quickly.

ADDIE: LIKE THAT IS IT? I WANT ALL THE DETAILS. ESPECIALLY THE ONES ABOUT A CERTAIN PROFILER WHO SEEMS VERY INTERESTED IN ALL THING'S DR SANKEY THESE DAYS. IF THE RUMOURS ARE TRUE, HE ALSO PLAYED THE HERO LAST NIGHT.

Savannah should have known her friend would know.

SAVANNAH: FINE YOU CAN HAVE DETAILS BUT MAKE IT TWO BOTTLES OF WINE AND GET JAVIER TO DRIVE YOU.

ADDIE: YOU GOT IT, GIRL.

Savannah smiled. She'd never thought her patient could become her closest friend or that by saving her life she'd be inheriting an entire group that made her feel like family. She loved her own family but her sister living away made it tricky for them and they'd never been that close. With her parents living on the coast now, she didn't get to see much of them either, but she knew they loved her and were proud.

Weekly phone calls still centred around her love life, or lack thereof, and how her time was running out to have a family of her own. As if she didn't already know all that, but love couldn't be forced. God knew she tried and look how that turned out.

"Savannah, what are your thoughts on this?"

She blinked as Percy addressed her and realised, she had no idea what he was talking about. She was so tired it was beyond comprehension but also too keyed up to sleep. "Well, Percy, I agree with you." She hedged her words not knowing what she was agreeing with but usually agreeing with his thoughts. He was a sound leader and insightful, and more often than not right in his assessment.

"Good, then it's agreed. We'll suspend admissions into the Neuro ward until a full independent investigation has taken place. I'll bring in another neurosurgeon on a short-term contract to help with what we have and go from there. We need to be seen as proactive after last night."

Savannah bit her tongue and regretted her daydreaming now. Closing her department wasn't what she wanted, short term or otherwise, but she'd agreed. Perhaps Percy was right, and it was the best option short term. They needed to get their house in order and make some changes. Last night should never have been allowed to happen and that it had reflected badly on her as the lead.

"What about Dr Farr?" Eddie Shand, head of Orthopaedics asked.

Percy pursed his lips and glanced at her with sympathy, which she didn't need. Or want. "Dr Farr has been released on bail pending a court hearing, but he's suspended for now."

"He should be fired!" Dr Shand stated, banging the table in outrage.

Orthopaedics tended to be arrogant bastards thinking they ruled the world because they brought in the big money.

"Dr Farr will be dealt with by the book so there are no comebacks."

"Fine."

"If that's all, we're finished here." Percy stood and the others followed suit, filing out of the room.

"Dr Sankey, do you have a second?"

She turned and nodded at Percy as the conference room door closed. "What's up, Percy?"

He smiled kindly and she remembered part of the reason she'd made the move to this hospital. Percy Gromadski was a good man and an even better leader.

"I wanted to let you know that I've arranged cover for you for the next few days. Take some time off. I know you must be exhausted and what you went through last night must have been frightening."

"Honestly, I haven't processed it yet. I knew Andy was spiralling but not to that degree. Have you spoken to Darla Jenkins?"

Percy wrinkled his nose in distaste. "No, but she's on sick leave.

No doubt her boyfriend's behaviour last night has put a strain on her, and with her being pregnant it's even worse."

"I'm sure, I actually feel sorry for her. Andy will never change but now she is tied to him by a child. At least I can get free when the finances are finalised."

"Very true. Now, your cover is coming in in thirty minutes. Why don't you do the handovers for your patients and then get yourself home? I don't want to see you inside this hospital until the investigation is over."

"But, Percy, those are my patients."

"I know. If we need you, we'll call and do a Zoom consult, but I want you as far away from this mess as possible. You're too good a doctor to get caught in this shit and let me tell you, changes are coming. I'm clearing out the deadwood now I have the chance."

Percy was kind but he was also cutting when it came to his first love, which was his hospital. He'd worked his way up to this role, retiring from surgery early when an accident had damaged his hand and left him with a tremor that ended his career as a general surgeon.

"Fine but make it quick. You know I hate being side lined."

Percy chuckled. "I do know that but think of it as having time to work on that paper you've been talking about."

That was a good idea, but she didn't voice it, instead, she made her way to her office and began the long process of handing her patients over to someone else. Something that didn't sit well with her, but she knew she had to do it.

Chapter Eight

Decker was still cursing himself when he walked into Eidolon. He'd kissed her hair for God's sake, that hardly screamed friends with benefits did it. He had no idea what had made him do it. He'd been surrounded by her scent, seen the look of utter exhaustion in her eyes, and lost his God-damned mind it seemed.

Pushing through the door for the kitchen, he saw Gunner making himself a ginormous sandwich and scowled. Gunner had always been a good man; he'd known that even when everything had pointed at him being the opposite. Decker had stuck by his profile and had been right. He'd never been so happy to be proved correct. Now since marrying Lacey he was even more settled.

"What crawled up your designer ass?"

"Nothing," he bit out trying hard to maintain his usual grip on his control.

Gunner chuckled and lifted his chin as he bit into the delicious-looking baguette.

Decker grabbed himself a water from the fridge and took a long drink. He'd never had trouble keeping his emotions out of the casual

hook-ups that consisted of his sex life. He had no use, or more importantly want, for them but now it was like all his icy control was slipping away.

"So, she got a name, or do I have to guess?"

Decker looked up, raising his brows, and stared down his nose at
Gunner with a look that would obliterate other men, trying to intimidate the man from furthering that sentence, but of course, Gunner
wasn't most men. He was in no way as big as some of the other
Eidolon men, but Decker worked out every day and was as a good a
fighter as any of them. He was lethal and he knew it and could take
just about any man in a room to his knees with a few well-placed
blows, and that was if he had to get physical. Mostly it never came to
that, his persona alone was enough. He cursed that it wasn't working
this time, but he'd helped shape these men to become hardened to
threats of any kind and they knew he'd never be a threat to them.
Their loyalty to him, and his to them, was the one good thing in his
life.

After Susie, he'd become so cold, so dead inside it had been easy
to remain remote, to show the outside world the monster he'd become
inside. His world had been stripped away leaving only pain so debili-
tating that he'd locked all his feelings away just to survive. Yet
Eidolon had shown him he could shed some of that mask and allow
friendship in, but never again would he risk loving someone so much.

"Deck, that shit might work with people who don't know you, but
you can cut that shit out with me. I'm not afraid of you."

No, the fucker just laughed harder.

"Asshole."

Gunner slung his arm around his shoulders and led him toward a
chair. "Come on, tell uncle Gunner all about it."

"Tell him about what?"

Deck groaned when Mitch walked in the room with Autumn, her
radar almost certainly picking up on gossip.

"Decker has lady problems."

Deck gave him a sharp look. "I said no such thing," he denied hotly.

"You didn't not say it."

"Oh, what's her name?"

Autumn sat opposite him, and he knew he was sunk if he stayed there. He stood abruptly and shot the three of them a stony frown. "For the last time, I do not have woman trouble."

He strode to the door as Mitch said behind him, "He totally has woman trouble."

Decker sucked in a lungful of oxygen through his nose and went toward his office. The last thing he needed was them getting up in his business and making this worse. Sitting at his immaculately clean desk, he powered up his computer. He had this under control, and he'd simply reacted to Savannah because she was tired, and it was a leftover reaction from what happened with her ex-asshole last night. He'd felt sympathy for her—yes that was it. He was merely showing empathy to a friend.

Yes, this was all good, he had control. With that in mind, he picked up the phone and called Aubrey. He needed to make sure Andy Farr was still in custody. That's what friends did, they looked out for each other.

"Hey, Aubrey, it's Decker."

"Hey, Deck, how are you?"

"Fine, fine." He didn't have time for small talk or distractions right now but needed to remain polite. "Listen, can you tell me if Andy Farr has been charged and what with?"

"Yes, he was charged with assault, endangering life, attempted manslaughter, and medical negligence."

"Is he still in custody?"

"No, he was bailed after his hearing this morning."

"I see." He clenched his jaw so hard he almost broke a tooth. What he wanted to say was fuck, but he remained outwardly calm.

"I know, but he has no prior convictions and surrendered his passport, so he isn't a flight risk and no immediate threat to life, especially as he's been banned from working until after his court date."

"That's okay, I understand. Do we have a date for that yet?"

"No."

He could hear Aubrey walking around, the background noise changing as she did. "We have to let the Crown Prosecution do their thing now and build a case. As soon as we have a date, I'll let you know."

"Thanks, Aubrey."

"So, you and Dr Sankey a thing now?"

He could hear the teasing note in her voice and knew better than to engage with a detective of her calibre. "Goodbye, Aubrey."

He hung up to her laughing and walked to his door. He needed to know where that fucker, Andy Farr was, and for that he needed Lopez. Which meant having a conversation he'd been avoiding since he'd insisted on fitting Savannah's alarm. That was the problem being surrounded by so many highly skilled operatives, nobody could get anything past them. It was worse now they were all married or shacked up because they had wives and they were even worse. Not even the FBI or CIA could compete when these women got even a sniff of a romantic connection.

He'd need to be clear on what this was if they asked and give them no room for scope or tittle-tattle. This was private and just sex and friendship, nothing more. Yet even as he said it, he was checking the locator on his phone that he'd slipped into her keys to make sure he knew where she was. Part of him felt like a creeper for doing it and not telling her. The other part that had seen far too many people die or end up in horrible situations, justified it as a precaution. She still had a stalker out there after all and this was simply a safety measure. That was the only reason, the only one.

He walked into the tech room and found Lopez at his desk working. He looked up and smiled and it was easy to see the change in the man. He looked like the baggage he'd carried alone for the last few years had lifted, leaving him free to be happy.

"Afternoon, Decker, what can I do for you?"

"I need a location on someone."

Lopez stretched his fingers and grinned. "Name?"

"Andrew Farr."

Lopez went still and then looked over at him, his hands still on the keyboard. "Savannah's ex-husband?"

Unreasonable and unwanted jealousy crawled up his throat at the thought of Lopez knowing so much about the woman he was about to start an affair with. He gritted his jaw and tried not to show any outward sign of the green-eyed monster riding him. "Yes."

Lopez leaned back and folded his arms over his chest. "Why?"

Decker could feel the protectiveness come over Lopez and felt irrationally territorial. Savannah wasn't Lopez's to protect, but then he had to remind himself she wasn't his either. Except, while they were sleeping together, she was. He didn't share and he took care of innocents, especially friends and Lopez had Addie.

"Because she and I are friends and after what happened with her ex last night, I want to make sure he doesn't go near her."

"Friends, you say?"

Decker swept an annoyed hand through his hair and glared at his teammate. "For fuck's sake. Yes, friend."

"Umm and is this the kind of friend that we share spit with?"

Fucking Waggs had blabbed. Goddammit, he should've known he couldn't hide fuck all from this lot. "Don't be juvenile, Lopez, just say what it is you want to know." He crossed his arms over his chest and waited, fighting the urge to throttle Lopez.

"Are you sleeping with Savannah?"

"Not yet."

"But you intend to?"

"We have an arrangement, yes."

"Does she know the score with you?"

Decker was interested to hear what the others thought the score was. "And that would be?"

"Oh, come on, Deck. We both know you don't do relationships

because you're still hung up on guilt from what happened to your wife and kids."

"Don't."

He spat the word out not wanting to hear any more. They didn't understand, they couldn't know, could they? None of them had ever lost the woman they loved or the children who meant everything to them and he prayed like hell they never did.

"Look, Deck, I know I don't understand and pray to God I never do, but I know about guilt, and it eats you up."

"This isn't guilt."

"Then what is it?"

"I don't want to talk about it."

"Fine, then let me say this. Make sure Savannah knows the score. She saved Addie's life and for that, I'll always look out for her. She's a good person and doesn't deserve to get her heart broken because you aren't prepared to open yourself up."

"Are you finished?" Deck felt like his tie was constricting him around his neck the more Lopez spoke, the Windsor knot he tied every morning suddenly feeling like a noose.

Lopez sighed and shook his head in resignation but thankfully dropped it. "Yes, just be careful with her."

"I would never hurt her on purpose."

"I know you wouldn't but that doesn't mean you won't."

"Message received."

"Right. So we need to locate Farr. That man is trouble. I already have a file started on him and he's into some shady shit."

"Can you send me everything you have on him and find out where he is? He got bail this morning and after last night I think it's prudent to keep an eye out."

Lopez cocked his head in question. "You think he's the one leaving messages on her door?"

"Maybe, but I won't rule anything in or out at this point."

"Okay, there he is going into his flat a few hours ago. I'll keep the software running so it pings if he moves."

"Thanks, Lopez. Can you email the file?"

"Yeah sure. FYI, Addie and Savannah are having a girl's night involving copious bottles of wine which means messy. I'm chauffeur but if you want to grab a drink later, I can get my mom to babysit Payton."

Decker didn't go out with the lads as much as he used to before they all got attached and liked the idea of a night in the pub. "Sounds good. See if the others want to join us, but no interrogating me about my sex life."

Lopez grinned and held his hands up. "Best behaviour."

Decker snorted. "Yeah, whatever that is."

He made his way back to his own office with his mind on Savannah. He wanted to see her, and tomorrow night sounded too far away. Maybe he could find a way to see her later, perhaps offer to pick Addie up as he wouldn't drink tonight anyway.

An idea formed as he delved deeper into Andy Farr's past. He didn't like what he was seeing. The man was on a path of destruction and involved with some very dangerous people and that put Savannah at risk. No, this would not do at all. He needed to make sure Savannah was safe for good.

Chapter Nine

Savannah opened the door and smiled at the six women on her doorstep, only one of whom she'd been expecting.

Addie stepped forward, a bottle of wine in hand and hugged her. "Hey, Sav, hope you don't mind but when I said I was coming here, these guys wanted to come and hear all about sexy Decker." Addie threw her thumb over her shoulder at Autumn, Bebe, Willow, Lacey, and Laverne.

"That's fine. As long as you have enough wine, the more the merrier."

Savannah laughed as each woman held up a bottle and she ushered them inside.

"Now this sounds like a party." Autumn smiled as they all swept into the living room and then through to the kitchen.

Jackets were discarded and Addie went looking for a bottle opener as she grabbed glasses for them all.

"I was going to order some food. What does everyone fancy?" Savannah laid a pile of takeout menus on the counter and then lifted her glass. "Cheers!"

The rest clinked glasses with her. "Here's to friendship in all its varied forms." Lacey waggled her eyebrows and Savannah groaned and raised an accusing eyebrow at Addie.

Addie held her hands up in surrender. "Hey, don't blame me, this was all Autumn."

"Wow, throw me under the bus, why don't you?" Autumn took a sip of her wine to hide her grin.

"Right, let's order food before we do this," Savannah demanded but secretly she was relieved to talk to someone about this. It was exciting and fun and outside her comfort zone. She wanted to talk to her girlfriends about it and over the last ten months, all these women had become like sisters to her.

Once they'd all decided on Japanese food and ordered, she sat in her favourite chair, curled her legs underneath her and waited.

"Well?" Bebe held her hand out, palm up for her to go on.

"What do you want to know?"

"Everything, starting with the hot kiss Waggs witnessed at the wedding." Willow topped off her wine glass and fanned herself.

Savannah had to admit that kiss was hot, but it also came with the swift bite of rejection straight after, and she needed to keep that in mind when she went into the fling with Decker.

"Well, first off, this is just a 'friends with benefits' situation. Mark has made it very clear that he doesn't want a relationship with me and there's no love involved, so if you have stars in your eyes, you'll be sorely disappointed."

Addie frowned but Savannah went on before she could speak, taking a gulp of wine for courage. "This is friends with benefits, nothing more, and he had a whole set of rules in place to make sure we don't get caught up in it. No, I haven't slept with him yet, and yes, that kiss was hotter than Hades but straight after, he was a dick to me. I'm going to give this a go because, well, you have eyes. The man is sex on a stick, but this is new to me, so I'm being cautious."

"Wow, that's a lot. You can take a breath now, Sav." Lacey patted her knee.

"So, he has rules?" Bebe asked as she crossed her legs, the wide-leg blue jeans looking amazing on her killer figure.

"Yes, no sleepovers and no feelings. No attachments at all."

"That makes sense after what happened to him."

Savannah felt the skin prickle in the back of her neck in warning and wondered if it was the light buzz she had going on thanks to the wine. "What do you mean?"

Bebe placed her glass down and leaned in close. "You don't know?"

"Know what?"

"Decker was married. He had a wife and son."

Savannah held up her hand. "No, stop. If he wanted me to know, he would've told me. I need to respect his privacy, so you need to stop talking."

Bebe nodded. "If that's what you want."

"I do. This is just friends with benefits, not true love." Yet even as she said the words, she wondered at her lie. It wasn't true love but it sure as hell was more than friends with benefits. She hadn't even tasted the benefit yet and she could already feel her mind drifting to him when she should be doing other things. When he'd kissed her hair today, it had taken everything in her not to lean into his touch.

A wife. He'd been married and had a son! It was hard for her to think of him as a father, but she knew like everything else he'd be a wonderful dad. Decker had more heart than he showed anyone, and she wondered if he hid it even from himself.

A knock on the door brought food, and the conversation soon turned to the wedding and Javier's proposal and Addie's wedding plans. The wine flowed and so did the conversation until Savannah began to yawn. She'd stopped drinking two hours earlier and had switched to water. Her tolerance was low at the best of times but when she was dead on her feet it was worse.

"Sorry, guys, it's all catching up with me."

"I'm not surprised after the last few days." Out of the Zenobi gang, Laverne was the one she knew the least. She was tall, slim, with golden blonde hair and deep blue eyes and she had what looked to be a permanent smirk on her face. Savannah knew that it was caused by Bell's Palsy and usually caused by an infection. It left patients with one-sided facial paralysis that once treated would get better but could leave a minimal amount of paralysis. She was a beauty with or without it and had a quiet confidence that made Savannah feel like she could handle any situation.

She wished she had even a third of that belief when it came to her personal life. Give her a scalpel and she was the best in her field, take it away and she was still the awkward girl she'd been in school.

"Waggs should be here in a minute and Gunner is coming for Lacey and me."

"Are they together?"

"Yeah, they had a boy's night at the pub, probably yapping about their cars and bikes and boring old man shit." Addie laughed and leaned against Lacey, who was as drunk as she was. The pair were going to have horrible hangovers in the morning, but life was for the living, and they were happy.

A horn beeped outside, and Savannah stood to go to the door, while Addie and Lacey giggled as they tried to find their bags and jackets. She pulled open the door, expecting Waggs or Gunner, and instead was greeted with the sight of Mark Decker.

"Mark, what are you doing here?"

He swept past her, and she caught the scent of musk and him, and inhaled without thinking. The effect was almost dizzying, and she swayed.

Strong hands caught her by the arms and he studied her. He looked down into her eyes, the intensity overwhelming. "Are you okay?"

She shook off the effect he had on her and pasted a wide smile on her face. "Yes, of course, just a little tired."

"Savannah." Waggs nodded as he moved past her and Decker in the doorway with Gunner behind him, both in search of their wives.

"Why are you here?"

"I offered to pick Addie up so Lopez could have a beer."

"You did?"

"Yes, I'm not much of a drinker so it was no trouble."

Savannah tried not to smile at the white lie, knowing Gunner was coming for Addie and Lacey.

He released her arms, and she felt the loss of his touch instantly. Oh, how she wished he could be here because he couldn't think of anyone else except her. That was fanciful and not in keeping with their arrangement and she had to remember that.

"Well, she's through there." She pointed toward the living room as Addie and Lacey came out with Gunner behind them looking amused.

Addie hugged her. "Thanks for a great night. Gunner is going to give me a lift home."

"Oh, I thought Decker was taking you home?"

Addie patted Decker's arm. "Be a doll and help Savannah clear up would you, please?"

She quickly intervened, not wanting him to think this was a set-up. "No, it's fine. I can manage, there's no need for Mark to help." She glared at Addie who just winked at her.

Decker cast her a look she couldn't read. "I'd be happy to stay and help you."

Savannah rubbed her hands together not sure what to do with them and worried if she didn't keep them busy, she'd launch herself at Mark. He looked hot tonight in his black t-shirt and dark jeans, his collarless leather jacket hugging his strong shoulders.

"See, he'd be happy to help you." Addie giggled and Savannah, now sober as a judge, tried not to roll her eyes and die of embarrassment.

"Come on you two, let's get you home before Savannah decides you need a frontal lobotomy for your craziness." Gunner ushered them out the door, followed by Waggs and the others.

She stood and waved them off for as long as she could, feeling the heat and presence of the man behind her the entire time. Finally, not able to avoid it any longer she turned, about to say he didn't need to stay but the look in his delicious brown eyes stopped her dead.

His hand on the door, as he closed it behind her and locked it tight, caged her body. His other hand cupped her neck and he pulled her to his chest, her palms landing flat against solid muscle.

A pulse in her neck pounded and she knew he could feel it against the thumb that swept over her throat. He looked like a caged predator, all hunger and heat, his natural dominance seemingly slipping the leash of his control, and she felt like prey.

"Are you drunk?"

Savannah closed her eyes at the demand, unable to speak past the desire flooding her veins.

"Look at me."

Her eyes shot open at his order, and she answered on an exhale. "No."

"Thank fuck."

Chapter Ten

The second he'd seen her standing in the doorway, with the light behind her like a fucking halo, he'd been lost. She looked so damn beautiful it was hard to breathe and then he'd caught the scent of her perfume, a light floral smell that seemed to control his brain and head straight for his cock. He was done waiting. He needed to feel her tight hot heat around his dick, to get her out of his system before she broke down every wall he had.

His head descended as she breathed out the answer he needed and then he kissed her how he'd dreamed of for days, weeks even. He swept his tongue into her mouth, controlling her movements with his hand on her delicate neck. She was so fragile and yet so strong; he'd seen the conflicting sides of her and wanted to taste them all.

He pulled away for a second, throwing his jacket to the floor and dragging her top over her head. He waited a beat, his eyes feasting on the lush curves of her breasts barely contained by the pink lace. She was everything he knew she'd be, perfect in every fucking way.

"You're so fucking beautiful."

His mouth was on her again, his lips tracing her neck, sucking on the pulse, which made his dick jerk in his jeans. He'd never wanted anyone with such a burning need it was almost painful, his cock aching to feel her.

He followed the curves of her neck down to her collar bone as her fingers threaded through his hair, her short nails digging into his scalp and making his dick jerk.

"Turn around."

He pinned her to her front door, her hands flat against the surface as he unhooked her bra and then kissed his way down her spine. His hand went to the front of her jeans, and he made swift work of the button and zipper before he dragged them down her toned, creamy thighs. His lips grazed the arch of her spine before he bit lightly on the ass cheek that begged to be squeezed as he fucked her hard.

This woman was consuming him without a single word. Her body was made for this, made for him and he wanted to take it all, everything she had to give him and never let go. His hand cupped her pussy and she gasped, her breaths coming fast, and it made him feel like a fucking hero. His finger slipped through her pussy lips, and he found her drenched with need, the feel of it only making him want her more.

Smoothing two fingers inside her, he nudged her legs apart with his knee. "Open your legs, beautiful."

Without question, she did as he asked, and he rewarded her with a caress of his thumb over her clit. Her moan of pleasure fuelled his desire. He wanted to taste her, but he wanted to fuck her more. Using his two fingers he fucked her sweet pussy and massaged her clit as her legs began to shake and her wetness coated his entire hand. He thought he'd come like a fucking teenager feeling it. She was a fucking vision and so open to him and he wanted to consume her, to own her.

"Oh, God, Mark."

He stood, his fingers never leaving her pussy and braced his body against her. "I've got you, Savannah. Let go. Come for me. Let me feel you."

Her cry was his answer as her knees locked and her thigh muscles shook, and she came. He'd never seen her look so beautiful. As she wilted into his hold, he swept her legs from under her and carried her upstairs to the room he'd left her in yesterday, his lips finding hers as she pressed against him.

He dropped her on the bed and quickly divested himself of his clothes. Her eyes travelled over his body, and he fucking loved the way she was looking at him, as if she wanted to devour him. Her eyes hungry, lips swollen and parted, he watched her breasts heave with every breath, the nipples a cherry-pink that begged for his mouth. With her hair around her shoulders, she looked like a siren straight from the storybooks of old.

She kept her eyes on his body as he rolled a condom down his sensitive cock and hoped like fuck he could make this last past a few minutes, but he was so fucking turned on he was doubtful.

Putting a knee on the bed, he crawled between her thighs and kissed his way up her smooth belly, smiling at the belly button piercing that showed a side to this woman he hadn't seen before. "That is sexy as hell."

Her smile was seductive. "Glad you like it."

He more than liked it but instead of answering her, he bent and dragged a distended nipple between his teeth. Her sharp inhale of breath turned into a whimper of pleasure as he flicked the sensitive nub with his tongue. She was so responsive, it was easy to learn what she liked, and he loved it.

Stroking his hard cock through her wetness, he clenched his jaw hard, fighting for control. The need to just slam into her was almost primal, but instead, he eased inside, her body hugging him like a fist, so tight and wet. He gritted his teeth and kept his eyes on her which only made it worse because she was looking at him as if he was the air she needed to live.

Her legs came up and wrapped around him as he sank deeper and then he was lost, his body taking over as he pushed into her before withdrawing, and he fucked her like his life depended on it.

Her hands, which held the lives of so many in their grasp, held on tight to his biceps, her nail marks dragging down his skin. The only sounds were of pleasure and sex, skin hitting skin, the smell of sex and her filling his nostrils.

He kissed her as she rocked back into his hips, finding a rhythm that was driving them both to the brink.

"Touch yourself."

He watched her hand snake between her legs where they were joined, and she moaned his name.

"Mark, I'm close."

"Do it, baby. Make yourself come on my cock."

His words seem to act like a detonator, and she came, squeezing his cock with her pussy so hard he thought he'd pass out from the pleasure. He came just as hard, the intensity almost blinding him as he filled her with his seed.

His arms shook from exertion, and he braced himself over her, catching his breath, their skin slick with sweat. He felt her arms go around him and stayed still inside her hold; his lips pressed to her neck. He wanted to stay there forever, to bask in what they'd just shared but he couldn't.

This wasn't what this was, and regret filled him. For the first time in ten years, he wished he could be the man who lay next to Savannah. To wake up and take her again, with the sweet feel of slumber making them lazy and languorous but he couldn't. The fact that he wanted to was a warning he should heed. He should stop this before it went any further, but he couldn't walk away now without having his fill of her, than fly to the moon.

Instead, he pulled away, guarding his heart against the look of hurt that crossed her face. He kissed her cheek and went to the bathroom to deal with the condom. Looking in the mirror, he saw a man he hadn't seen in ten years, a man who'd been so broken he thought he was dead, and it terrified him, but not enough.

Cleaning up, he walked back into the bedroom and saw she'd pulled a sheet over her naked curves. It was a crime to cover such perfection and yet he was glad she had as he dressed quickly. He didn't need any more temptation.

Savannah was an open book, and he could see her valiantly trying to act casual, but he knew this wasn't her. She'd done this for him because she wanted him. Selfish bastard that he was, he was willing to let her.

He sat on the bed, not wanting to leave her yet but knowing he had to go. His hand snaked under the sheet, and he palmed her breast, his finger and thumb rolling the nipple and her breath hitched. So fucking responsive, she drove him wild.

"Did I hurt you?"

She shook her head, a sexy smile curving her full lips. "Not at all, I enjoyed it."

"Me too." He wanted to say more, to explain why he had to leave, to tell her that he wanted nothing more than to break his own rules and stay but that wasn't what this could be. "You working tomorrow?"

"No, I'm on leave until an internal investigation has been done."

He frowned, his fingers stilling on her perfect body. "Why?"

"Percy is trying to protect my reputation by keeping me clear of the fallout."

His hand wandered down her belly, to her clit which he circled with two fingers before dipping lower and finding her wet and ready. Fucking hell, she was going to be the death of him. "I never got the chance to taste you."

He dragged his fingers through her wet heat and up her belly before he rubbed them over his lips and sucked them into his mouth. Her taste was like nectar, sweet and tangy and he wanted more.

"I didn't get to taste you either."

His dick jumped, fully hard and ready to go, but he fought for dominance over his libido. "I guess we have something to look forward to for next time. That is if you want to do this again?"

"Absolutely. Friends with benefits seems more fun than I ever imagined. I think it's my new favourite thing in fact."

Jealousy, hot and swift, hit in him the gut and he wanted to go and find the future man who'd get to touch her and kill him. She was his, to touch, to own, and he wouldn't let another man have her, but he had no rights. Except for the ones he had for now, for as long as this lasted.

"But for now, you're mine and I don't fucking share."

"Neither do I."

"Point taken. While this lasts, we only have each other." He wanted to say more, to demand she say she was his, but he didn't.

"Fine by me."

She yawned and he ran a finger over her cheek. "Get some sleep. I'll set the alarm when I leave."

He kissed her once more as her eyes began to close and left the room before he did something stupid like crawl back into bed with her and hold her while she slept.

Chapter Eleven

Savannah stretched out like a cat, curling her toes as the aches in her body reminded her that last night hadn't been a dream. Hugging the quilt cover to her nose she inhaled the scent of Mark's cologne on her sheets and a stupid grin spread from ear to ear. She'd known the sex would be good between them, chemistry like they had couldn't be faked, but it had been so much better. Mark Decker fucked like a god; he should have statues made of him. Jeez, the Queen should give him a Knighthood for services to women. She giggled to herself at the crazy thoughts. The only sting in the tail had been him dressing straight afterwards and leaving.

She would've given almost anything to fall asleep with him, but that wasn't part of the deal and she'd agreed to it. Now she wondered if she had what it took to be a fuck buddy. Oh, she'd been full of bravado after telling him how she wished she'd done it sooner, but the truth was, she wasn't sure she could keep her head and heart separate with this. He was just so intense. He made her feel like nobody else existed and that was dangerous for her heart. It wouldn't be so bad if he was an asshole everywhere else, but apart from the needling and the incident at the wedding, he'd been sweet and kind, protective even.

Knowing she couldn't lie in bed all day playing out every scenario, she threw her legs out of bed, wandered into the bathroom, and turned the shower on to hot. The air seemed cooler today, the hint of an early autumn in the air. She loved this time of year the scent of apples filling the air and the hint of winter around the corner.

Dressing in a pair of olive-green paper bag trousers and a cream t-shirt with a leopard print heart in the middle, she pulled her hair into a ponytail and added white Vans to her feet.

Stomach rumbling as she went downstairs, she remembered at the last second the clean-up she still had to do from last night. Not that she'd change the fun night she'd had with the girls, her friend-ship with these women was priceless and something she hadn't realised she'd missed until she had it in her life.

Stepping into the kitchen, she was surprised to find it spotlessly clean. All the empty food boxes were gone, and her glasses were clean and put away. Smiling, she realised Mark must have done it before he left last night. A warm feeling swept through her, and she did her best to tamp it down. This meant nothing, it was just Mark doing what he'd said he would and helping her out, nothing more.

Grabbing herself a cup of coffee and a banana, Savannah went to the couch and fired up her laptop. She had time on her hands and if she didn't want to spend it stressing about her patients and second-guessing every decision the new doctor might make, she had to keep busy.

She spent the rest of the morning working on her clinical paper before she realised she needed some data that the lab at the hospital would have. If she swung by her office, she could just log in quickly and check on everyone from afar.

She parked her car around the back by the mortuary, in the hope of avoiding Percy and the lecture she knew she'd receive. Her mind on the paper and her patients, she wasn't conscious of the shouting until she rounded the corner. Zeroing in on the three men, she recognised Andy and frowned as she ducked back behind the dumpsters, an inner instinct taking over that she didn't recognise. A primal warning tickled the back of her neck as her heart began to thud in her chest. Taking out her phone, she silently opened the camera and began to video the three men. She had no idea why she was doing it, just that it seemed like the right thing to do. Plus, the alternative was to move from her hiding spot and then they would see her, which, judging by the appearance of the two men, wouldn't be a good thing for her. Something about this seemed off and the hair on the back of her neck rose again in warning.

A gasp escaped her, and she put a hand over her mouth to stop the sound as one of the men pulled a gun and held it on Andy. Her ex-husband was an asshole, but she'd never want to see him hurt. Not knowing what to do, she carried on filming, knowing if she moved, she was dead. She wished she could get closer to get a better look at their faces but all she could see was the side of the one man's face and the back of the other as he waved the hand at Andy.

What was he doing there anyway? He was banned from the premises until the investigation was concluded and his trial finished.

"You were warned, doctor. You either got us the money or you paid with your life."

Andy held up his hands in submission, looking nothing like the confident man he'd once been. Savannah's mind whirled with possibilities at the words. Was Andy in trouble financially? He had plenty of money and no overheads. Had he fallen so far down the rabbit hole that he was hanging out with men like this now?

A loud unmistakable pop made her jump, the phone shaking in her hand as Andy fell to the ground, blood exploding from his chest like a river. Another pop followed as he lay on the ground and his body jerked as a bullet slammed into his head.

Fear almost knocked her over and she moved unsteadily, kicking an empty pop bottle at her feet. She saw the eyes of the two men swing in her direction. Shit, shit, they'd heard her and now she was in big trouble. She knew if she stayed where she was, she was dead for sure so she did the only thing she could and ran.

She heard the men behind her, one telling the other to get the car and he'd get her. Not happening, dickhead, no way was she ending up like her ex. She could hear running footsteps behind her as she darted around the side and found the ambulance exit for the mortuary. She punched in her code with shaky fingers and knew she didn't have the time to fuck it up as the footsteps were coming louder now. Breath quivering in her chest, Savannah sighed as the light turned green and then she pulled the door open and slipped inside, pulling the door closed.

Around her, people were going about their jobs with no knowledge of what had just occurred outside. Whoever these men were, they knew the security camera didn't cover that area of the hospital or maybe that was Andy's doing. Passing a lab tech, she smiled and kept her head down as she walked fast towards the lab. Rounding a corner, she flattened her body against the wall as she saw one of the men walk in and look around, and she knew he wasn't going to give up without a fight.

His hand hung loosely at his side and the other was tucked into his jacket with a gun in it. It was obvious he didn't want anyone to see him but more so that he wanted her. She ducked into the viewing room that held just three chairs, a row of small cupboards and a single unit for the body of the deceased. Closing the door silently, she made sure the curtains on the glass window were closed and sank to the floor in the corner.

Her hand shaking so bad she could hardly grip her phone, she dialled Mark. He'd know what to do and, in this second, he was the only person she could think of that she wanted to make this right. The phone rang and she tried to calm her breathing as she listened to the sound of her heart in her throat, as almost deafening, paralysing fear crippled her.

"Hey, Savannah." His warm, deep voice crashed over her and almost took her under the torrent of feelings.

"Mark, I'm in trouble."

"What's wrong?"

She could instantly hear the change in him, he was taking control and she needed that. "They killed Andy."

"Who killed Andy?"

"Two men and now one of them is here looking for me."

"Where are you?"

"I'm hiding in the mortuary viewing room at the hospital."

"Lock the door and don't let anyone in until I get there. Keep this line free and hold tight. I'm on my way."

"Okay, hurry."

"Savannah, it's going to be okay."

"Okay."

"I'm hanging up so I can arrange back-up."

"All right."

The click of the call ending was loud in the silence, and she felt so alone as she clutched her phone so hard her fingers cramped. Mark was coming he'd be here soon, but as she heard screams a few minutes later and then gunfire, she wondered if he'd be too late.

Chapter Twelve

"Lock the door and don't let anyone in until I get there. Keep this line free and hold tight. I'm on my way."

"Okay, hurry."

Decker paused, taking the time to reassure her even though all he wanted to do was run out the door. A feeling he couldn't place gripped him hard. "Savannah, it's going to be okay."

"Okay."

Jesus, the fear in her voice almost slayed him. She was one of the calmest people he knew, not prone to dramatics and he was around the coolest of people on a daily basis.

"I'm hanging up so I can arrange back-up."

"All right."

Decker hung up the phone, not wanting to kill the connection but needing to concentrate and knowing that listening to the fear in her voice would distract him. She didn't need that from him, she needed him to keep his head. He ran to the tech room and slammed open the door. Lopez's eyes came to him in shock.

"Lopez, call Aubrey. There's a situation at the hospital." He explained the rest in short succinct sentences as he began to prepare mentally, keeping a rein on the fear that was riding him so he could do what was needed. Lopez got to work calling Aubrey and he ran for the gym where the team were working out. Gunner, Waggs, Reid, Liam, and Mitch stopped dead as he ran in, their eyes falling to him.

"Savannah's in trouble. Two men just shot her ex at the hospital and now they're after her."

As the men sprang into action, all of them heading for the weapons room and gearing up in tactical clothing and grabbing what they might need, Decker checked his phone. He wanted to call her back, but he could tip off the people hunting her. Lopez ran in, handing out comms and followed them to the Husky, a protected patrol vehicle and mobile command centre.

"Aubrey is talking to Percy and locking the hospital down. That means the mortuary is locked down from the rest of the hospital."

"Tell her we're not waiting."

"Already did, she said she'd have it approved, as the nearest armed response is at least fifteen minutes out."

"Good." He didn't care if it was approved or not, he was going. The thought of Savannah in that situation was almost unbearable and if he wasn't dead, he'd kill her useless ex-husband for dragging her into his shit.

Liam jumped in the driver's seat as Lopez went back to command central. He'd co-ordinate from there, using all his toys and tools to guide the team. He'd also get in touch with Alex and Blake and let them know, although with Alex out he was the highest-ranking, and this was his call anyway.

"What do we know?" Reid demanded as he clipped his vest tight around his middle.

"Not a lot. Savannah called me five minutes ago and said Andy Farr was dead and she was in trouble. Two men were after her and she was hiding out in the viewing room of the mortuary."

Gunner tapped an iPad looking device in his hand. "Lopez patched us into the hospital cameras. We have eyes on the front of the Mortuary, but the back is a black zone."

"Can we get eyes inside?" He needed to see as much as he could before they went into this.

"Negative."

Liam turned a corner at breakneck speed, and he hung on to the overhead grab hold.

"We go in as two man teams. Mitch, you go with Waggs and cover the back, infill through the fire door and clear the labs." Decker pointed to the schematics of the mortuary and tapped his earpiece to connect with Lopez. *"How old are these blueprints?"*

"They were filed with the council two years ago so should be pretty accurate."

"Good. Reid and Liam, you go in and clear the left side of the building. Gunner and I will take the right."

The men nodded. This was a drill they'd practised a hundred times, and they could do it in their sleep but suddenly it was different. Someone he cared about was in danger, but he knew he needed to keep a cool head.

The Husky came to a halt outside the lab, and they all jumped out. Aubrey had beat them to it and was cordoning off the area and approached as they exited.

"Sit rep?"

"We still have people inside the building."

"How many?"

"Six lab techs and the mortuary assistant."

"Any sign of the gunmen?"

"No, but there's a chance they made it out without us spotting them. When the hospital locked down, there was a bit of a panic and lots of people ran."

"Okay, we'll take it from here."

Aubrey nodded and stepped back; she knew what they were capable of.

"Go time, boys."

The six of them approached the mortuary building. Mitch and

Waggs disappeared around the back, and the rest of them moved either side of the front door.

"*In position,*" Mitch said over the comms.

"*Execute, execute, execute.*"

As one unit, they breached the glass doors and, laser-focused, he and Gunner began clearing the right side of the mortuary. He found the mortuary assistant huddled under, her desk.

"Go." He waved her behind him where he knew the path was clear to the exit for her and she ran.

He could hear Reid and Liam as they herded the lab techs out of the way.

"*Left side clear,*" Reid confirmed.

His eyes on the door where he knew Savannah was hiding, it took everything in him, every ounce of training, to not rush to her because that was how people ended up dead and he had no intention of that happening. He saw Mitch and Waggs headed his way and they nodded to the autopsy room. Deck tipped his head in acknowledgement.

Only one door was left, and they hadn't seen any sign of the gunmen. He could hear Lopez leading them and giving them intel as they moved and, in his gut, he knew they'd missed them. He just prayed that they hadn't found Savannah first.

With his hand on the door, he nodded to Gunner. Opening it, Gunner stepped in and swept the room, but his eyes were only on the woman curled up in a ball on the floor. He crossed to her in a second as she scrambled to her feet, and he wrapped his arms around her.

The sigh of relief that shuddered through her was met by his own relief. He stepped back as Mitch declared the building clear and his eyes swept over her, trying to catalogue any injuries and thankfully finding none.

"Are you okay?" He cupped her face and tipped her head to him and saw how pale she was. She'd be going into shock any minute now and he needed to get her out of here so he could check her over properly.

"Yes, they didn't find me." She exhaled shakily and he brought her into his chest and held her as she clung to him.

Easing away, he wrapped her in his arms and walked her towards the front exit. He knew Mitch and Waggs had found Andy, and Waggs had confirmed his death.

"Let's get you looked over."

"I'm fine, Mark."

"I'll be the judge of that."

Mark saw a waiting ambulance had been pulled around to the side and he led her that way and left her with the ambulance crew, who she knew well if the way they greeted her was any indication.

"Mark!"

He turned as she called him, and she hopped off the gurney and held out her phone for him to take. "I recorded as much of what happened as I could."

He looked at her in shock. Even terrified, this woman had the foresight to know what to do. He took it from her hand and without a thought for what he was doing or what it meant, he hauled her to him and kissed her as if she was the oxygen he needed to survive. Her body leaned into his and she clutched his biceps, holding on. Breaking the kiss, he looked down at her and felt his heart thud hard in his chest.

This woman was special, and way too good for what he was offering her, but he had nothing else to give her and was too selfish to walk away from what she so freely offered. The only thing he could give her was sex and justice, and he'd make sure he gave her both.

The fuckers that had stalked her and threatened her had gotten away this time, but little did they know they'd just made a deadly enemy—the deadliest in fact.

Chapter Thirteen

She felt like she was having an out of body experience as she watched the police coroner load her ex-husband's body into the back of the black ME van. She felt nothing, not sadness or fear, just a complete numbness. Her gaze moved to Mark as he spoke with Gunner and Reid. She could still feel his arms around her and wanted nothing more than to go to him and have him wrap her up again and give her the feeling of safety that she wasn't sure she'd ever feel again.

"All set, Dr Sankey."

Hannah the paramedic had checked her over, even though Savannah had told her she was fine. She hadn't had the energy to argue and had let them do their checks.

"Just make sure you rest. Shock is still an issue. You should probably make sure you aren't alone after an experience like that."

"Thank you, Hannah." Savannah smiled even though it felt rigid and false on her face. She had no doubt she was in shock; she knew the signs, but she just wanted to go home and crawl into bed and pretend this had never happened.

As she hopped off the back of the rig, Mark walked towards her.

His eyes wandered over her body, not in a sexual way but assessing her.

He held out his hand to her and she took it. "How you holding up?"

He was tall, towering over her and she wanted nothing more than to bury her head in his chest and let him take the weight of it all. She'd never been so tired and knew it was the adrenalin crashing hard.

"I'm okay." He raised a brow at her, and she shrugged. "Tired, I guess."

"Let's get you home and you can get a shower and some rest. Aubrey is going to come by later and get a statement from you. The video is a huge help for them to get started identifying the men."

Savannah didn't want to think about those two men. Every time she closed her eyes, she relived the moment Andy fell to the ground dead as if in slow motion. Tears pricked her eyes as Mark helped her into a car and clipped her seat belt like she was a helpless child.

He gripped her chin and turned her to look at him. "It's going to be all right, doc." He kissed her gently and she swallowed a sob, his tenderness and care battering her defences.

The drive home was short and when she got there Lopez and Addie were waiting for her. Her friend took her in her arms the second she saw her. "Oh my God, Sav. I was so worried." She stepped back and held Savannah away, observing her.

"I'm okay, Addie." She was so used to being the caretaker and it felt odd to be on the receiving end of it—not bad just different. She swayed slightly on her feet and Mark wrapped an arm around her hip to steady her.

"Let's get inside before you fall down."

He guided her inside to the couch and then crouched. "I'm going to make some tea. Will you be okay for a minute?" His hands rested on her knees, and she wanted to reach for him. But they weren't a couple, and yet, she was fighting not to lean on him.

"That sounds fine, thank you."

He gave her one more look before nodding once and moving away. Instantly, the air felt colder, as if by him walking away he'd taken warmth she needed away too.

"Here, have this." Addie wrapped a blanket around her shoulders and Savannah smiled.

"Thanks."

"Want to talk about it?"

Savannah shook her head. "I don't think I can." She rolled her lips between her teeth as her voice broke.

Addie hugged her, rubbing her back. "I know, honey. I know."

Savannah leaned against her friend and closed her eyes for just a moment, and the image of Andy came into her mind. She didn't love him anymore, but she'd never wanted that. It was hard not to still care for him, even after all he'd done, to see him die so suddenly and in such a way shook her. God, his child would grow up without a father, his parents had lost a son, and his girlfriend, no matter how much Savannah disliked her, had lost the man she loved.

"Here, take this."

Savannah opened her eyes and took the steaming tea, the heat warming her frigid hands.

She blew on the strong tea before taking a sip and winced at the sweetness, she didn't normally take sugar but knew a lot of people thought it was good for shock. "What happens now?"

Mark took the seat to her left and turned slightly toward her but kept a physical space between them that she wanted to cross but felt unable to. "The police will identify the men and start their investigations."

Addie snorted. "Don't tell me you won't be looking into this."

"Already are. Lopez has a file on Andy Farr, and we're looking into his dealings with these men, but I can tell you this. None of what we've found so far makes what happened today a surprise. He was in bed with some seriously bad people and up to his neck in debt to a loan shark called Benny Vasquez."

"Is that who killed him?" Savannah shuddered at the thought of what Andy had been involved in.

"No, but I suspect they worked for him."

How had she not known any of this? How long had it been going on? Was he involved in it while they were married? All of a sudden, it all became too much, and she knew she was on the verge of a complete meltdown. She had to get out of there so she could break down in private. She didn't want her friends or Mark to know how close she was to falling apart.

Throwing the blanket off, she stood abruptly. "I need to take a shower. Excuse me." Her voice wobbled as she spoke, and she fled the room as the tears erupted and a sob escaped her lips.

Reaching her bedroom, she quickly stripped off her clothes. She felt the urgent desire to get anything that had touched today off. She felt dirty, unclean, and rushed into the bathroom needing to shower and clean the filth of the day from her body, even as she recognised that it was her mind that was upsetting her. Savannah ramped the heat up in the shower as she stepped under the hot spray.

She scrubbed her skin as sobs bubbled up. She let the grief and fear and all the emotions from the day take her as her legs gave way, and she sank to the floor of the shower and cried.

Chapter Fourteen

Decker closed the door on Lopez and Addie after assuring Adeline that he'd stay with Savannah and make sure she was taken care of. The truth was they wouldn't have been able to make him leave. He heard the shower start and then the sound of unimaginable pain as he took the stairs two at a time and her sobs could be heard through the door.

Without a second thought, he pushed through the door. Steam filled the bathroom. Pain lanced through him as he saw her collapsed on the shower floor, her body sagged against the tile as wracking, gut-wrenching pain stole her breath from her body.

Opening the door, he shed his shirt and stepped into the cubicle. She didn't even look up, she was so lost in her pain, her hiccupping gasps breaking his heart in two. Crouching, he wrapped his arms around her back and threaded his arms under her knees as he lifted her and carried her towards the bed. Her arms came around his neck and he felt her burrow closer to his skin. He set her down with a kiss on her temple and quickly dried her with a fluffy white towel, goosebumps dotting her skin where she'd scrubbed at it.

Pulling back the quilt, he pulled a t-shirt he found in her drawer over her head and stepped back.

Her eyes went wild and scared, panic evident in her expression as fresh tears hit her cheeks and she held her hand toward him. "Please don't leave me."

Decker shed his clothes until he was standing in his boxer shorts. "I'm not going anywhere, doc."

He climbed into the bed and pulled her into his arms, so she was lying half over him and pulled the quilt over them both. Holding on to her in the fading light of the day, he gave her his strength, knowing that she needed him and, instead of the usual fear it would bring, he felt only grateful he could be the one to give her what she needed.

Her body was soft and perfect against his, as if she'd been made to fit there and he took the pleasure in holding her that he'd wanted last night and hadn't allowed himself to indulge in. Selfish bastard that he was, he wanted this with her. Not the pain and fear she was feeling but this closeness.

Her sobs slowed and her heaving body began to quiet, her breathing evening out until he knew she was asleep. Decker stayed listening to her breathing, feeling her body move silently against him and knew it would be easy to let down all his walls for this woman. But even if he did, where did that leave them? He couldn't give her marriage and a family; he'd had his chance at that and blown it. He wouldn't risk that again, not even for the beautiful, sensual, intelligent woman who was stealing parts of him without his consent.

His thoughts depressing, he switched his mind away from things he couldn't control and concentrated on those he could. The men that had killed Andy Farr were deadly and he had no doubt in his mind that Savannah was in grave danger until they were found. Lopez had found them shortly after they'd cleared the building heading north and away from the hospital. CCTV had shown them escaping in the panic with staff members, but they wouldn't give up.

People like that didn't leave loose ends and that was what Savannah was. Really, he should wake her and get her away from this house. Only the security he'd set up and the fact that Liam and Blake were watching the house gave him the peace he needed to give her this time to grieve and get herself together.

This was a reaction to everything she'd been through in the last few days, both the attack by Andy in the operating theatre, which felt like it had happened years ago, the tense operation she'd carried out on the boy, and then witnessing her ex-husband dying, all on top of her exhaustion. It was too much, and her body and mind had done what it was meant to do and shut down, protecting her in the only way it knew how.

He lay awake holding her while she slept, enjoying the intimacy as he watched her sleep. She was so beautiful. He'd seen that from the first time he'd laid eyes on her. Her warm smile had hit him like a sucker punch, and he'd hated it because it terrified him. Not since his wife had a woman affected him like that. If he was honest, even Susie hadn't had that effect, their relationship had been different.

Childhood sweethearts, their relationship had evolved into love, and he'd adored her, their sex life had been good. How he felt when he looked at Savannah though was sharp like a blade. A sexual attraction like he'd never felt before, and then the guilt had hit and he'd lashed out at her.

Now he knew her, knew how sweet and kind she was, how intelligent and driven, it only made his attraction worse until he'd had to have her. The only way to keep what they had safe was to keep it locked up in this fucking arrangement.

Her body stirred in his arms, and he looked down into her eyes to see them flutter open and she gave him a smile that cut through his bullshit and made him inhale sharply. A look he'd never imagined being on the receiving end of again.

"Hey."

"Hey, you."

Decker rolled so he was lying in between her legs, his hard cock pressed against her pelvis, arms braced either side of her head. She was so stunning it took his breath away. He felt like a starving man finally being given food. She nourished his soul in a way he couldn't explain.

"I'm sorry about earlier."

She looked away in embarrassment and Decker wouldn't stand for her taking any blame for her reaction. "Hey, look at me, doc." He pressed his fingers lightly against her jaw to turn her to face him. His eyes met hers and he could see the spark was still there but had lost its brightness and he hated that for her. "You aren't to blame for anything that happened. No matter what you had done, they would've killed him and you, too. Anyone who's been through the crap you have in the last few days would've reacted the same."

"You wouldn't have."

Decker smirked. "Yeah, well, I'm not anyone, I'm me."

Savannah raised a brow as her hands began to travel over his back, and he fought the shiver at her touch. His dick was so hard being this close to her.

"Oh, is that right? And what is so special about you, Mr Decker?"

Fuck! Her flirty tone and the touch of her fingers on his skin was driving him crazy.

He bent his head and rubbed his lips against her neck. "How about I show you?"

Her body arched deliciously beneath his and she moaned as he bit her neck, his teeth skimming the sensitive skin.

"Good idea."

He brought his lips back to hers and kissed her gently, his tongue sweeping across her open mouth. Her hand moved down his abdomen and she pushed her hand into his boxers as she gripped his swollen cock hard, making him hiss in pleasure and throw his head back. His eyes came back to her, and his gaze swept down her face. Bending his head, he nipped at her nipple through the thin cotton of her t-shirt, the tight bud begging for his touch.

Her hand stroked him, and his hips bucked, pre-ejaculate soaking her hand.

"Mark, I need you."

Urgency filled the room as he pulled her t-shirt over her head, leaving her deliciously naked beneath him. Her warm wet heat cupped his arousal and he kissed his way down her body. Much as he wanted to feel her tight pussy around his dick, the need to take care of her first was stronger.

Pushing her legs wide, he kissed the silky soft skin of her inner thigh as he kept his eyes on her. Her fingers threaded through his hair as his tongue swept through her sex, the taste of her making his cock flex with need.

"You're so fucking gorgeous, doc."

Her response was a whimper as she tugged on his hair.

He circled her clit with his tongue as he slid two fingers into her body, before adding a third. The sound of him fucking her with his hand as he devoured her with his mouth filled the room. Her cries and whimpers were his new favourite sound and as her pussy clenched around his fingers hard, her body stilled before he felt her clit spasm against his tongue.

Grabbing his wallet, he rolled a condom down his hard length as she watched with hooded, satisfied eyes. She lay replete where he'd left her, legs still spread wide for him to see her pink sex glistening from his tongue and her climax. Decker stroked his cock once as he bent a knee into the bed and moved back between her thighs.

"You look like fucking sin right now."

Her hands caressed his thighs before he hooked her knees over his forearms. Hauling her up, so only the top of her back was on the bed, he rubbed the tip of his cock through her wet before pushing into her. His eyes closed, she felt too good, too perfect, and he needed to stop, or he'd blow his load like a fucking teenager.

Her muscles rippled around him, and he opened his eyes to see her lips open in pleasure. How had he gone so long without this and how would he live without it when this was over? It was a question he didn't have an answer for, so he pushed it out of his mind and began to fuck her slowly. Building her pleasure with every demanding slam of his body into hers.

"Touch yourself."

Her hand moved between her legs, and she circled her clit with two fingers as he watched her, his gaze moving between her hand moving in a frenzy to where his cock disappeared into her, before coming back to her face. She was so expressive, so into this, showing no shyness or hesitation. She was taking what she needed and giving him the same.

It was a sensory overload, and he knew she was close and held on tight, his movements becoming uncontrolled as he rammed into her body like a wild man now. His mouth found hers in a messy kiss and he felt her body clamp down on his so hard he almost saw stars as he came harder than he ever had in his life.

His body sagged onto hers, sweat dripping off them both as they held on and he kissed her face, her neck, anywhere he could touch and the realisation that this was so much more than fuck buddies left him feeling completely fucked and having no clue how to handle it.

Chapter Fifteen

The smell coming from downstairs swirled around her as Savannah sat up and pushed the covers back. After the shitty things that had happened the last few days, it seemed crazy that she couldn't drag the smile from her face. Last night, Mark had fucked her three times before they'd fallen into an exhausted sleep with her wrapped in his arms.

Somehow, something had changed between them. Although no words had been exchanged, she could feel the new closeness between them. As she dressed in blue jeans, a cream shell top, and a longline pale pink cardigan, she could feel the aches from the sex. Without doubt, it had been the hottest night of her life. Part of her felt guilty for feeling so satisfied when her ex-husband was lying in the morgue, but she couldn't help herself.

Walking down the stairs she found Mark, sitting at her table, drinking a coffee, and reading his iPad. He looked up when she entered the room and smiled as he held out his arm for her. Savannah walked into his embrace, and he pulled her down on his lap.

His eyes instantly dropped to her lips, and she could feel the hunger she felt reflected in him. "Good morning. Did you sleep okay?"

Her arm around his neck, the other hand skimmed his jaw as she brought his lips closer, the stubble of his jaw a reminder of how it had felt between her legs. She wanted to tell him it had been the best sex of her life and she'd slept well knowing he held her, but she knew it would cause him to panic and flee. Mark Decker had secrets and pain in his past that she knew nothing of. She wanted him to trust her enough to tell her, but she knew she couldn't rush it, so she kept it flirty and fun.

"I would have but some sex-crazed deviant kept waking me up."

"Sex-crazed deviant, hey?"

His hand stroked over her thigh and came to rest on her rib cage just below her breast. His touch drove her crazy, she felt like an addict wanting her next fix already.

"Um, yes."

"Well, you're the doctor, maybe you can prescribe me something for it?"

"I might have an idea."

She couldn't stop her lips from skimming his cheek and her teeth tugging on his earlobe.

A loud knock at the door broke the bubble they were in, and she wanted to shout at whoever it was to go away so she could stay here in this haven with just the two of them.

Mark tapped her butt for her to stand. "Duty calls."

Savannah went to stand but he pulled her in for one last kiss which made her toes curl it held such promise.

"Until later, doc."

"Later."

Going to the kettle, she made herself busy making tea, not even questioning why she was letting Mark open her front door.

"Hey, Deck."

She heard Alex's voice and turned around to greet him. "Hi, Alex."

She held the coffee pot up and saw him nod. "God yes please, I feel like I haven't slept in ten years."

Savannah grinned. "I take it Clara still isn't sleeping?"

Alex sat down at her kitchen table and rubbed his hands over his face as she handed him the coffee and he sipped it and sighed in pleasure. "No, colic and it's horrific. I swear terrorists have nothing on the sight of your child crying for no reason and having no clue how to fix it."

Decker pursed his lips. "Try white noise. It worked with Milo when he was a baby."

Savannah stared in shock and Alex looked at him in surprise. "Thanks, Deck. At this point, I'll try anything. Evelyn is shattered."

Savannah turned back to the kettle to busy herself, and to stop herself from asking about Milo. Was he the son her friends had mentioned? Did Decker have kids and if so, why had he never mentioned it? A thought struck her, and she prayed she was wrong and that the man she was coming to care for, was falling for, hadn't suffered the worst kind of agony.

Pasting a bright smile on her face, she turned and brought her tea to the table. "So, Alex, apart from coffee and advice, what brings you over?"

Alex cast a glance at Decker and a message seemed to pass between them. Her heart began to beat faster as she gripped her mug so hard it was a wonder it didn't crack.

Mark looked at her. "We identified the men who killed Andy."

Savannah looked between the two of them, growing impatient with the way they were hesitating. She'd been upset yesterday but she wasn't a delicate flower that couldn't handle the truth. "And?" She rolled her hand to try and encourage them to speak, the testy tone of her voice making the corner of Mark's lips tip up.

"They belong to the Cavendish crime family."

Savannah looked at Alex for his reaction and saw him watching her. Savannah shook her head. "That means nothing to me." She rubbed her temples, a headache beginning to form.

Mark leaned toward her and took her hand. "The Cavendish crime family is the biggest crime family in Europe. They own the Elysian Casino group, the Cavendish fashion house, and several other legitimate businesses but it's their illegal dealings that have made them the billions they're now worth."

"I don't understand, Mark. If you know this, why aren't they locked up?"

He sucked in a breath through his nose and pursed his lips. "It's not as simple as that and nobody has ever managed to get them into court for any charges to be brought." He squeezed her hand and leaned in closer. "No witnesses ever live long enough to testify, and evidence always goes missing."

A gasp escaped her as she realised the magnitude of what they were telling her and felt her tea roll in her belly as nausea and fear assailed her. "They killed Andy and I recorded it."

Mark nodded slowly. "Yes."

Her gaze went to him as the severity of what he was saying hit her. "Am I in danger?" Her knuckles were white as they gripped his hand and she made to let go, but he threaded his fingers through hers and held tight.

"I won't let anyone hurt you, doc." Mark turned to Alex. "Can you give us a sec?"

Alex stood. "Sure." Savannah watched as he slipped out the front door before her eyes moved back to the handsome man in front of her. He really was devastatingly beautiful and the air of dominance that surrounded him made her body tingle with the memory of his touch. How was it she was aroused by this man at this moment? Her world was crumbling around her, and all she wanted was to get Mark naked again and feel his touch on her skin.

His eyes fell to her lips and the room hummed with electricity. "You're such a fucking distraction, Savannah. How is it, when I'm giving you this news, all I can think about is how you taste on my tongue when you climax, how you feel when your cunt clenches around my cock?"

Savannah drew in a breath at his dirty talk, words which would've made her cringe with shyness in the past but with him, there was only this pull between them. Deep down she knew that a connection like this didn't last, that it burned bright and white-hot and then fizzled to nothing. Mark was the hottest sex of her life and she wanted to enjoy every second of it before he got bored and she only had memories. She just needed to remember to protect her heart in the process.

"I know the feeling." The admission was out before she could stop it and she was rewarded with a sexy smirk.

Mark stood and walked to the kitchen and began to rinse his mug. "You can't stay here. This house is no longer safe enough. You'll stay with me until the men who are after you have been taken care of."

There was so much to dissect in that one sentence she didn't even know where to start. His dominating nature was sexy as hell mostly, but she wasn't a weak wimp to be bossed around and have her decisions made for her. Neither was she a fool. She knew that Mark and Eidolon knew way more about this than they let on and her safety was at the forefront of his demand. She wasn't that stupid girl who ran through a dark house with a serial killer chasing her. Eidolon were the experts in their field, and she respected that. If she was in danger, she at least wanted to be part of the discussion about what happened to her, even if she knew she'd do as he'd demanded.

Savannah stood, knowing she had to word this carefully but not prepared to back down. Her hand reached for his forearm as he straightened from loading her dishwasher. He turned and pulled her between his strong thighs as he leaned against the counter and she let him, the feel of his body against hers too good to step away from. Every hard ridge, and one particular hard length, frying her brain.

Swallowing, she pushed past her desire for him. "Mark, I understand I can't stay here, I really do, but I don't think it's a good idea for me to stay with you, either."

He frowned and she could see he was pissed off, felt the tension radiate through his body and wanted to soothe him. Her hand stroked over his biceps, and she loved his strength.

"What the hell does that mean?" He pulled from her hold, and she let him go.

"Just that with this thing between us, it might make things difficult. You said yourself we have rules, and they're a good idea. I need to protect my heart from becoming involved with this." She rolled her finger between them. "I can go and stay with my parents."

Mark turned and the arrogance that she'd seen before was there. "Absolutely not, you'll be putting a target on their backs."

Savannah sighed wishing he could see what she was saying. "Fine, I can stay with Addie then."

"And risk Payton?"

Shit, she hadn't considered that and was still grasping the reality of the situation. "Fine, a hotel."

Savannah sat down heavily in the kitchen chair and watched as Mark prowled toward her. He crouched and she remembered how he'd taken such good care of her last night and before that with the security and the paint on her door. He was a good man, just a little arrogant and a lot bossy.

"Do you think I can't protect you?"

"What? No, of course not. I know you can, but I don't want to complicate things."

"Savannah, you will stay with me. I'll keep you safe. We can continue exploring this attraction and amend the rules to suit our new situation."

"How?"

"Well, instead of the sleepover rule we put a time limit on us. When the threat is over, we go our separate ways as friends with no hard feelings."

"What if one of us catches feelings?" The question slipped out before she could stop it.

Mark brought her fingertips to his lips and kissed them as he gave her a sexy smirk. "Don't worry, Savannah, I won't fall in love with you."

She stayed silent because she wasn't concerned about him falling in love with her but her with him. Clearly, he had no inclination or feelings towards her except sexual. Could she do this and keep her heart safe? She didn't know but she was about to find out because there was no other way. "Okay, good. I need to pack my stuff up then."

"Leave it. Alex and Blake will do it. Just grab what you need for today."

Now it was settled she sensed an urgency about him. "Mark, how bad are these people?"

"The worst, doc, the absolute worst."

How had this happened? Damn Andy!

With her laptop bag and handbag over her shoulder, she went to open her door, but Mark stopped her with a hand on her arm.

"Let me go first."

Savannah blinked slowly as understanding and reality hit her. Mark opened the door after speaking into a comm unit she hadn't seen him put in his ear. The door opened and Liam and Alex flanked her on either side as she was rushed to the car, Mitch opening the door for her with a warm smile. He then jumped in the driver's seat as Mark got in beside her and the car began to move.

A sudden thought hit her as the black Land Rover, with privacy glass and a dashboard that looked like mission control, sped away from her beautiful home, her haven. "Is Andy's girlfriend and unborn baby safe?" She may hate the bitch, but she'd never want to see her hurt, and never an innocent child

He glanced across at her. "Yes, we had her moved to a safe house this morning."

"Oh, okay."

She gazed out of the window as the car pulled into Eidolon HQ and the security gate closed behind them. This was surreal, and yet, as the images of her ex dying and a man with a gun chasing her appeared in her mind, she knew this was her new reality. At least for now.

Chapter Sixteen

"You're so fucked!"

Decker glanced across the room at Waggs who was sitting at the desk opposite him. He frowned at his friend. "What the hell does that mean?"

"That's the third time you've zoned out today. What the hell is going on with you, Deck?"

Waggs was bang on with his assessment. He was fucked and zoning out because he couldn't stop thinking about how soft Savannah's skin was or how amazing she felt when her lips were on him.

He sat forward and glanced at his watch. It was only four in the afternoon, and he was done. He usually worked until seven or eight, not having a reason to go home and pushing his mind to work was what he did. It was his escape but now she'd invaded that, and he didn't know what to do. Maybe talking to Waggs would help him gain some perspective. "I let slip about Milo in front of Savannah this morning."

Waggs brows rose, and he sat forward in his seat. He knew Decker never spoke of his wife and son. They all knew what had happened, he'd never really made a secret of it, but he never spoke about what had happened or them. It was too painful, so he kept it locked away in a mental vault.

"What did she say?"

Decker blew out a breath and linked his fingers behind his head. He'd lost his suit jacket and rolled his sleeves up, which was as relaxed as he got at work unless he was working out or on a mission. "Nothing. Alex was talking about the baby having colic and I said white noise helped Milo when he had it."

"So, she doesn't know what happened or who Milo even is?"

Decker shook his head. "No. It's not like that between us. We're just friends with benefits."

"Really? She doesn't seem like the kind of woman who would settle for that."

Another sigh escaped him, and he dropped his hands to lap. "She isn't but the attraction between us is off the charts. We've fought it for too long. I'm hoping we can get it out of our systems while she stays with me and go back to being platonic friends afterwards."

"You really think you can walk away from a woman like Savannah?"

No, he didn't but he knew he had to. She was everything he could ever ask for, and in another time or place, she could've been his everything, but he had nothing left to offer her. His heart was a shrivelled lifeless organ in his chest. It might as well have been buried beside his family. He cared for her; he could acknowledge that. She was kind and funny, clever, brave, and so damn sexy, and she challenged him in ways nobody else ever had.

Just that thought made him feel guilty. His Susie had never challenged him. She'd been the opposite of Savannah, a stay-at-home mom with no ambition, except to be a wife and mother.

Savannah was driven and successful, his equal in every way but to love her was something he could not and would not risk. "I have to walk away, Waggs. I have nothing to give her."

"You sure about that? Because from what I can see, you're already doing it."

Decker scowled at Waggs. "Meaning?"

"You're bringing her into your home, you're protecting her. You care, Deck, and that's okay. Look, I know what happened to you is the worst thing imaginable, God knows if it were Willow or AJ, I wouldn't be able to live through it, but you did and you have a lot to give. Don't turn your back on a second chance out of misplaced guilt."

"What if it's not misplaced? What if the guilt is right where it should be?"

Waggs stood and headed for the door. "I don't believe that. You're one of the best men I know, and you would've died to protect the people you love. What happened was tragic, but it was an accident."

Having said his piece, Waggs closed the door leaving Decker with his thoughts. Waggs was wrong, he could've done more to protect them. He could've been where he said he'd be and then they'd still be alive. His selfish need to show the world how brilliant he was had gotten his family killed.

Taking out his phone, he opened the camera roll and went to his family album. He didn't do this often. It was too painful to see the still images of his wife and son so happy when he'd never get to experience it in person again. He scrolled to the last image of the three of them together. His son in his arms, his arm protectively around Susie as she smiled up at him, her belly round with the daughter he never got to meet.

The look of love and happiness was on all their faces, a time of laughter and freedom, but he remembered that picture being taken. They'd been at a birthday party for a friend's child, and he'd been itching to leave and get back to the office so he could follow a lead on a case.

He'd taken it all for granted and paid the ultimate price, and he'd never risk it again. Savannah might be everything he wanted but he wouldn't fall for her, he owed his family better than that. They could never move on, and neither should he be allowed to.

He could, however, enjoy the brief time he had with her and

make sure she was safe from the Cavendish family. She deserved that. To be free from a threat so she could go on and meet a man who'd love her how she deserved to be loved.

His jaw clenched and his fist tightened on his phone at the thought of another man laying his hands on her perfect body. Jealousy, hot and ugly, swamped him and he stood, having to physically push it away. Slipping his phone into his pocket, he rolled his sleeves down, fastened his cuffs, and slipped on his jacket.

It was time to head home. He was getting nothing done here anyway. He could hear Savannah laughing with Autumn in the office as he walked down the corridor and fought the smile the sound brought to his face. He stopped at the door and watched in silence as she played on the floor with Maggie, Autumn and Mitch's little girl. Technically she was Mitch's stepdaughter, but no one would ever know it. She adored him and he adored her.

Savannah was helping Maggie do a large picture puzzle and the look of joy on Savannah's face made his gut tighten and his heart skip a beat. Savannah would be an amazing mother one day. Her kids would be so lucky to have her and the lucky bastard who got to share it with her better appreciate just what he had, but it wouldn't be him. Regret consumed him and he had to swallow it down, so it didn't choke him.

At that second, she looked up and smiled at him, and it was like being hit by a truck. The blinding joy on her face was so genuine it would've made a lesser man buckle and beg her to never leave him. How her dick of an ex-husband had let her get away was a mystery he'd never solve. If she was his, he'd spend every day making sure she never had a reason to leave him.

"You ready to go already?"

He stepped into the room and grinned at Maggie before greeting Autumn. "Yep, not getting anything done so we should go. I can try and work from home later."

"Okay, let me grab my laptop from the conference room."

"Goodnight, Autumn."

"Bye, Savannah. Bye, Deck."

"Goodnight, Autumn." He winked at Maggie who clapped her hands and giggled. "Goodnight, Maggie."

He followed Savannah out and went to let Liam and Reid know they were leaving. They'd be guarding his house that night from outside. The threat from the Cavendish family was real, and now they were on Eidolon's radar they'd be dealt with.

Reid was in Alex's office on the phone.

"Yeah, you too, sunny. See you in the morning, babe. I love you."

Deck lifted his chin. "She okay with this?"

"Yeah, fine. Clay is coming over with Hattie in a few weeks, so she's busy getting the house ready."

"That's cool. How is Clay?"

"Good. He and Hattie are expecting and won't be able to fly out for New Year so they're coming now."

"That's awesome. Clay is a good guy."

"Yeah, the best."

Reid stretched as he stood and swept his hair back. "You ready to go?"

"Yeah, if that's okay with you and Liam."

"Sure, Liam is in the garage playing with his new toy."

Decker rolled his eyes. Ever since he and Taamira had been trying for a baby, Liam had been buying up mini versions of the cars they drove for his child.

"He does know it takes at least a year before they can walk right, and this one isn't even conceived yet?"

Reid chuckled. "Yep, the man's obsessed."

"Who's obsessed?" Savannah asked as she caught up to them and they walked toward the door.

Decker scanned the area, and Reid followed suit as they logged out of the building.

"Liam is obsessed with knocking his wife up."

"Ah, I see."

Decker took her bag and helped her into the Land Rover, and she rewarded him with a soft smile that made his chest heave and his dick twitch with arousal.

"You seen Decker's place yet, doc?" Liam asked as he jumped in the driver's seat.

"No, I'm excited to see it, though. Autumn said it's gorgeous."

God, he needed to fuck her out of his system and quick before he caved and did something monumentally stupid, like beg her to stay with him. "Can we just go and stop acting like this is a fucking sleep-over. This is work and nothing more."

Reid and Liam exchanged a glance which he ignored, as well as the hurt look on Savannah's face.

"No need to be a jerk, Mark."

"Don't start, Savannah. I'm not in the mood for your shit."

Reid cut him a look from the passenger's seat which said he was being a dick. He *was* being a total dick and knew it, but he shouldn't be feeling this excitement at the thought of having her in his space.

She glanced at him and pointed to her chest in outrage. "My shit?"

He wanted nothing more than to lay her back and fuck her until neither of them could speak or think. She was fucking beautiful when she was angry. It made him hard fighting and bickering with her, like it was some twisted foreplay.

Savannah sat back with a huff and refused to look at him the rest of the ride to his home. The silence in the cab was filled with judgement and he hated it. If they were alone, he knew both his friends would've reamed him out for being a knobend.

The car pulled to a stop on his drive as close to his door as Liam could get, and Reid jumped out, slamming his door hard in a testament to his anger. Decker got out and went around to open Savannah's door while Reid and Liam flanked the front entrance, which they'd opened, so she could go straight inside. Before he could get there, she opened it herself and jumped out and headed for Liam and Reid.

He caught up and grabbed her arm. "You will not get out of the car without me there again, do you understand?"

She glared at him and yanked her arm from his grip and moved inside.

"Dickhead." Liam shook his head with a smirk.

Decker ignored it and slammed his front door so hard, the house rattling from the force. He set the alarm and turned to see her arms folded, her face like thunder as she waited for him to tell her where to go.

Fuck, she was something else. He'd never felt this all-consuming desire for someone. It was as if they were opposing energies being pulled together by a force neither could control. Arousal bit at his skin as he walked toward her, backing her into his home office.

The pulse in her neck beat wildly and he saw her eyes darken with desire as her tongue came out to swipe across her bottom lip. She was as turned on as he was. Fuck, she got off on them fighting too.

"On your knees, Savannah. I want to fuck that disobedient mouth."

He held his breath as he waited to see if she'd comply with his demand. This side of himself wasn't one he'd shown her before.

With her eyes never leaving his, she slowly sunk to her knees and his breath shuddered out at the sight of her on her knees for him. He could see the defiance on her face but more than that, the excitement. "Unzip me."

Her hands went to his pants, and she slowly unzipped him, sliding her hand inside and pulling his boxers down enough that his hard cock bobbed free.

"Suck me."

Her tongue came out and swept over the tip as her hand gripped him hard at the base and his knees almost gave way. Her tongue was fucking perfection, but he needed more. Sliding his hands in her hair, he gripped hard and angled her head as he slid his cock across her lips, the pre-ejaculate leaving a sheen on her skin. As she opened her mouth, he pushed inside, and heaven awaited.

Savannah didn't suck his dick for him. She did it because she liked it, because she wanted it as much as he did. As his tip hit her throat and he stilled, holding her still. With his cock in her throat, her eyes on him, he wondered how he'd let her go.

Pulling her sharply to her feet, he spun her around and pushed her over his desk before pulling her pants down to her thighs. Testing her with his fingers, he found her wet with desire and chuckled. "You're fucking soaked."

"I need you, Mark."

His hand gripped her hair. "And you'll take what I give you."

Releasing her, he grabbed a condom and rolled it on before he rubbed his cock through her wet sex. Without any finesse, he pushed inside her, the hiss of breath at the intrusion making his balls draw up. She was so tight and hot. He could feel her walls flexing around his cock and knew this would be quick.

He slammed into her, taking her hard, the desk smacking against the wall as she held on. His hand moved to her clit and teased the sensitive nub as his thumb breached her ass, and she came so hard he couldn't hold back his own orgasm. He pumped his climax into her hard, his moan echoing off the walls at the same time as her cry of pleasure.

Decker slumped against her back, his lips finding her neck as she turned to him with a smile.

"Are you okay? Did I hurt you?"

"I'm fine, Mark, and that was hot as fuck."

He rested his head against her back, his dick still inside her and never wanted to move. "I'm sorry for being an asshole."

"If all apologies come with that, then feel free to let your inner asshole out to play more often."

And just like that, she forgave him, and they were okay again. How would he resist falling in love with this woman?

Chapter Seventeen

"**L**et me show you to your room."

Savannah had barely finished straightening her clothing when Mark spoke, his tone back to being cool but friendly, nonetheless. She had no idea what had caused that spectacular lack of control from him resulting in her getting thoroughly fucked against his desk, but she wasn't complaining. It was probably the single sexiest thing ever to happen to her. Mark Decker was one hot, dominant, alpha male, and her body responded to him in a way she didn't recognise. If he kept this up, he'd ruin her for other men for the rest of her life. Who was she kidding, he probably already had.

"Here you go. The bathroom is across the hall. I have my own, so you'll have your privacy."

Savannah looked around at the beautiful double bedroom that looked like a luxury hotel suite. Decorated in a champagne gold and plum colour, it was stunning and just her style. "Thank you, Mark, for doing this. I know I'm putting you out and if you change your mind, I can make other arrangements."

She faced him and gave him an out she hoped he wouldn't take, because the truth was, she didn't feel safe with others like she did him. A trust had formed, a bond, and while she had no idea what he felt for her, she recognised she was falling for him. It would be healthier to leave and stay with one of the others, but she wanted this time with him no matter the cost.

Mark hung his head a second, his hand on the door frame before his eyes met hers and she could see restraint in them. He walked toward her, and she forced her feet to stay still and not lean toward him, seeking his touch like a desperate woman.

A gasp escaped her when his arm went around her waist and he pulled her, so she was flush with his hard body. His head dipped and she looked up into a face that was too handsome for words. He made her needy and hungry, her actions that of a teen with her first crush, not a grown woman with a successful career and an ex-husband. Her hands braced on his chest, she leaned back slightly.

"You're not going anywhere. I've given you this room but let me be clear, I want you in my bed for the duration of your stay here, but that's up to you. In no way do I see you as putting me out or as an inconvenience. I want you here, doc."

His voice softened with sincerity at the end and Savannah got the feeling he was waging some internal war with himself. "Okay, Mark, but promise you'll tell me if it gets too much? I never want to be a burden to someone."

His lips dropped to her neck and skimmed her pulse and she shivered. "How could anyone ever consider you a burden?"

"I mean it, Mark."

He sighed and his head came up and she fought the desire that blazed under her skin. This man was like her personal Kryptonite. When he was around and looking at her like he was now, all reasonable thought left her brain.

He released her and stepped back. "I know, and I'll tell you if it becomes an issue. Now, would you like to get some dinner? I can cook or order out."

Her eyebrows rose in surprise. "You cook? This I have to see."

"Prepare to be amazed."

Savannah followed him out of the room he'd allocated her and passed several closed doors, idly wondering which one was his.

"Mine is the one next to yours, in case you're wondering how to find me later." He turned and winked, and she blushed as he read her mind.

They went down the stairs, and she couldn't keep her eyes still as they took in the gorgeous house. She'd hardly taken it in when they'd arrived, too pissed off at first and then too busy having her mind blown by her sexy protector.

The kitchen was drool-worthy with large, gloss grey cupboards and stainless-steel appliances for every activity known to man. The main kitchen island had a waterfall edge with seating for six people that she'd die for.

"This house is amazing! How long have you been here?"

Mark ducked his head in the fridge and began pulling things out and placing them on the side. He held up a packet of chicken breasts. "Harissa chicken and roast veg?"

"Sounds wonderful."

He began to season the chicken with a paste, and she sat at the island and watched before asking if she could help. He pointed to the veg and she began chopping the peppers ready for roasting.

"In answer to your earlier question, I've been here five years. I moved to the UK ten years ago when I began working for Jack. I had a flat in town at first, but this came up at a steal because of a foreclosure with the developers and I couldn't resist. The fact it was fully decorated was a bonus."

"It's beautiful. Didn't you feel the need to change anything to how you wanted it?" She knew, as gorgeous as this was, she would've changed things, to put her stamp on the house so to speak.

Mark slid the chicken into the oven and washed his hands again. "Not really. I work too much to worry about shit like that."

Savannah pushed the veg his way and he took over. "Do you want a glass of wine?"

She cocked her head. "Are you having one?"

Mark shook his head. "No, I don't drink a lot."

"Then no, just water for me, please."

He handed her a glass of water and sat at the island with her as delicious scents of cooking food surrounded them, making her mouth water.

"Tell me about the Cavendish family." If she was going to run scared, she wanted to know who from.

"Wow, straight in with the big guns." He stayed quiet and she remembered he was a talented profiler and could probably out wait anyone.

"I just need to know what I'm dealing with, Mark. I don't work well in the dark. I need facts, they keep me calm."

He pursed his full lips, and she got distracted by the images they wrought. "I understand. Shall we go into the lounge and relax for a bit? This will be a while."

Savannah picked up her water and followed him into the lounge, which had been decorated in greys and blues, with warm wood tones on the floor, and matched the rest of the ground floor. A large sectional couch framed a gorgeous contemporary fireplace, which housed a massive TV above it.

Mark took a seat and tugged her hand, so she was seated beside him before he angled his body towards her, closing the distance but not touching her. It was as if he needed her close enough to touch, even if he chose not to.

"The Cavendish family is made up of Winston Cavendish and his two sons, Damon and Gideon."

"Wait. I know those names. Are his sons doctors?"

Mark frowned and shook his head. "No, Damon is a barrister and Gideon is running the family business, at least the legal side of it. Winston remarried after the boys' mother died and had a third son. His name is Carter, and he's the driving force behind the drugs, prostitution, guns, loan sharks. You name it, he's involved."

"Yes, that's it. Damon Cavendish represented a huge lawsuit against Nex Pharmaceuticals for not being honest about the side effects of the epilepsy drug they created. But I thought you said they were a crime family."

Mark nodded his head in understanding and held up his hand. "I know and it is, because Winston still holds the reins and while he's around, he protects Carter and makes his other sons do the same. My personal opinion is Damon and Gideon want no part of it but are being forced to protect their younger brother."

"So, Winston is making his sons be criminals?"

"In a roundabout manner. They're driven, rich, and from what I hear, completely cutthroat in business and in the courtroom. Winston's second wife is from a family with ties to the Italian Mafia and I think Winston has been dragged into it, and so have his sons."

"Wow, that's awful. Can't they find a way out?"

"I have no idea, and that's not really our problem. At the moment, it's getting the target off your back and putting the men who killed Andy in prison."

Savannah shifted closer. "But surely if we approach the brothers, they'll help us?"

"Why? They don't know us. Why would they help us?"

"Surely we can appeal to their better nature."

"Don't assume because they aren't as involved as their brother, that these are good men. They still protect him and his illegal dealings, and hundreds of people die because of it. These aren't good men that will do us a favour just because we asked."

"Surely we could offer them some incentive?"

"Savannah, that isn't what Eidolon does. This isn't our usual remit. It's only because of who you are that we're involved."

Her enthusiasm left her in an exhale of breath. They were helping her out and she was trying to tell them how to do their jobs. He'd said she wasn't a burden, but she could already tell she was.

"Hey."

He lifted her chin with his finger, and she glanced away, not wanting him to see the defeat in her eyes. She was already missing surgery and her patients. Being a doctor was who she was, and she wanted her life back. More than that, she wanted this feeling of help-lessness to be gone. She fixed things, so sitting back and letting others handle her shit was grating on her nerves.

"Look at me, Savannah."

What was it about that tone that made her comply with his every command? She had no clue, just that she couldn't disobey him if she tried. Her eyes moved up his face until she was looking at his deep brown, intense gaze.

"We'll find a way to fix this. Jack is on his way home. We'll fix this so you're safe and free to live your life without terror or the spectre of what you witnessed hanging over you any more than is necessary."

"I'm sorry you got dragged into this."

"You didn't drag me anywhere. We're friends, remember? It's what friends do."

He pulled her into his arms and kissed her head as he held her tight, and she wished beyond anything else that this moment was real. That he felt something more for her, that they were just another normal couple having a meal together and relaxing.

Pulling herself together, she pasted a smile on her face and put some distance between them.

"You promised to amaze me with your cooking skills."

"I did, didn't I."

He took her hand and led her to the kitchen with a smirk on his face and a more relaxed manner as if whatever had been bothering him earlier was gone.

And amazed she was when an hour later they were seated at his dining table which, as with the rest of the house, looked like it came straight from a home décor magazine.

Savannah sat back and patted her full tummy. "That was amaz-ing, Mark."

"I'm glad you enjoyed it."

She had, far too much for her own good. Mark was fun and inter-esting, and they talked about so many things. His job, her job, the friends they had, her family, politics, movies, music but he never once mentioned his own family. There was a story there she knew, and the name Milo kept going over and over in her head, but she never had the courage to bring it up. Something inside her knew that he'd close the door firmly in her face at this point if she did.

Mark held a pain deep inside him that he shared with nobody, and it was linked to that name and his family. Her heart ached to soothe his pain and learn more about him and his past, but they weren't that. They were fuck buddies and it felt too intimate to bring up, and coward that she was, she didn't want to tempt him into bringing his walls down when they were just beginning to lift, showing her a glimpse of the man she wasn't only sleeping with, but falling for.

Chapter Eighteen

Mark lay with his hand behind his head in his bed and stared at the ceiling. She'd been in his home three days, living with him, cooking alongside him, sharing his space, and he already dreaded the day it would come to end. He turned over annoyed that his arms ached with the emptiness of not holding her and punched his pillow.

Every second she was in danger ate at him, but it was also the reason she was there, and he realised he liked having her in his home and his life, and not as a friend with some fucking fantastic benefits. Not twenty minutes ago, she'd kissed him goodnight after he'd fucked her until they were both replete and gone to her room next door.

He hadn't pushed her to sleep with him all night and knew she was trying to respect his initial set of rules, but goddammit, he wanted her here. He rolled onto his back, kicking the sheet from his torso, the rub of cotton over his dick enough to wake that eager part of his body. He'd been hard from the moment he'd seen her months ago and getting her out of his system was failing spectacularly. He wanted her more now than ever and not just naked, he wanted to be around her.

Jack had arrived back in the country two days ago after a delay at the airport and was already fully up to speed with everything. He'd floated Savannah's idea to lure one of the Cavendish brothers into helping them and had been met with surprise. It was rare he went out on a limb or asked for anything. His team had never seen him with a woman before. Even his one-night stands had been kept separate from his work life.

Now he was asking them to help a woman everyone could see he was fucking, and he'd been caught more than once watching her as she worked in the conference room on her paper by one of the guys. It was unlike him, and it was unsettling at best.

Jack had agreed this was a case that would be long-winded and involved and, while it wasn't something Eidolon could commit to, he'd ask Shadow to take it up. The team that made up Shadow were as trained as them, all highly skilled and deadly individuals, but unlike Eidolon they weren't all ex-military or law enforcement.

Some were ex-criminals looking for redemption, others had spent their lives walking the line between good and bad and living in the grey so long it was comfortable to them. Others had made fucked-up decisions that had changed the course of their lives for good. But all were on the side of innocence and determined to take people like Carter Cavendish down. And who better than a team who didn't exist, with people who'd had their identities wiped clean from existence.

The clock on his nightstand read three am and he realised it had been two hours now he'd been lying there waiting for her to come back or change her mind while he acted like a lovesick fool. Throwing back the covers, he stalked into the hall and listened for a second at her door. He paced away and spun on his heels and bit the bullet. If she wouldn't make the move, he would.

Opening her door, he saw the slash of light through the curtains fall over her body, the luminescence making her seem ethereal and highlighting the perfection of her skin. She went up on one elbow as he approached the sheet falling to reveal the t-shirt she was wearing in bed.

"Is everything okay?"

Worry tinged her voice and he cursed inwardly for scaring her. "No." He bent and scooped her up in his arms, her body moulding to his as she clung to him. He turned and walked back to his bed and set her in the middle before he got in next to her and hauled her over him, so her body was like a human blanket while he encased her in his arms. "Now everything is okay."

He felt her smile against his chest and fought his own.

"You could've just asked me to stay in here."

"I did."

"No, you told me where your room was, that's not the same. I'm trying to navigate my first fuck buddies' relationship, Mark. Hints won't cut it for me."

"Fine," he said sulkily, still not happy that he needed her this way and not prepared to put a label on how he felt, because then he'd have to make a decision he wasn't ready for and end it. "You sleep in my bed until this thing between us ends."

She was silent for a long time and he wondered if she'd fallen asleep, but he sensed she was awake. "Does it have to end?"

He closed his eyes against the regret that slammed into him at her question and the temptation to say no, to tell her how much she meant to him, how she was saving him one second at a time from a loneliness he'd never acknowledged. Knowing he owed her more than a perfunctory answer he held her tighter and kissed her head. He needed to tell her about Susie and Milo and the baby girl he never got to hold. She deserved to know how fucked up he was and why he didn't deserve to have the love of a woman like her before she did something crazy like fall in love with him or see something she thought was worth saving when he knew there was nothing to be saved.

God knew it was bad enough he was falling in love with her when he didn't deserve the dirt under her shoe. He could handle loving her and not having it reciprocated but he couldn't cope with risking it and lowering his walls and losing her like he had his family. Or worse, her loving him and him letting her down, and he would. He was too selfish, too driven, and most definitely unworthy.

So, he began to speak, knowing there was a good chance she'd get up and walk from this room and never speak to him again after he confessed how he'd killed his family.

"I met my wife in high school."

He felt her tense against him and then relax, listening intently to his words.

"Susie was perfect. Kind, loving, beautiful, and she wanted me. I have no idea why she chose me, but she did, and I loved her. I adored her. We got married right out of college and had a son, Milo. He was the most amazing kid. He loved trucks and Lego and had the kindest heart. He'd cling to my leg when it was time for me to go to work because he didn't want me to leave and would run to me when I got home."

Decker drew a steadying breath as memories assailed him and he let them come, feeling safe in her arms to indulge. "When Milo was two, we moved to New York for my dream job with the NY office. Susie hated it, but she stayed for me. She was a wonderful wife, but Milo and I were her life and she struggled to make friends and missed home. I knew she hated it. It was the only time we fought but she'd always give in to my needs over her own."

Savannah stroked the skin of his chest offering comfort and he clasped her fingers and kissed them before laying her hand back down but keeping a hold on her.

"I was working a huge case, the biggest of my career and I was so wrapped up in it. Susie was pregnant with our daughter and was struggling with the New York heat. I said I'd take Milo to day care, and she could get some rest, and that weekend we'd go home and see her parents."

The next words almost burned with the regret he felt. "We had a break in the case, one I'd made and ended up catching a killer that had been on the rampage for months. I was so fucking proud of myself, so arrogant. I forgot to take Milo to day care, so Susie drove him. On the way, their car was t-boned by a truck. They were killed and my little girl never took a breath."

He waited for the recriminations and disgust that he felt about what he'd done, and she remained silent.

"Oh, Mark, I'm so sorry. I can't even imagine that kind of loss and I deal with it every day."

He held her body close and tried to lose his fear in the touch of her body against his. "I expect you detest me now."

"What? No, of course not. What happened wasn't your fault. It was an accident and if you'd been driving, it could've been you killed."

"I wish it had been, then they'd be alive."

Savannah sat up and he could see tears on her cheeks for him glisten against the dawn light. "Listen, I know you probably don't believe me, but this wasn't your fault and punishing yourself for it won't bring them back. Yes, maybe they would've lived, but maybe not and all of you could've died and the countless lives that you've saved over the years would be lost too."

He lifted his hand to swipe the moisture away and his gut clenched. How was he going to let her go? And yet he would, he must. "Don't cry for me, doc. I don't deserve it."

"Of course, you do. You lost your family, the people you loved, and you're still grieving. Most probably you will every single day for the rest of your life, but don't stop that from letting you honour them by living. You have so much love to give, Mark, and even if it isn't me, you should open your heart up to love again."

"Why don't you hate me?"

"I hate you? For what?"

"For letting them die because he was selfish."

"I don't hate you, Mark, I..."

He reached out and covered her lips with his, to stop her words.

He couldn't hear them; he could never hear them because he wasn't worthy of them. "Don't."

"Okay, Mark."

He kissed her like she was his saving grace, and she was. He could just never have her because if he lost her too, he'd never survive it.

Chapter Nineteen

Savannah didn't know how it was possible but a week after Mark had made his heart-breaking confession, she had to acknowledge that she was head over heels for him. His honesty and the raw grief and love he still felt for his wife and children shone a light on the soul of a man so good he wouldn't cut himself the slack he deserved to move on. She understood survivor's guilt, she dealt with it every day with her patients, but ten years was a long time to punish himself for something that wasn't his fault.

She wondered how much fear of feeling those emotions again and risking it happening again controlled him and her heart ached for him. Something had changed between them that night and the week since had been beautiful. They drove into Eidolon together every day and she worked on her paper while he worked in his office. They ate lunch together, sometimes with the other team members and other times alone, just enjoying the comfortable silence.

In the evenings he'd cook, and she'd sit and talk to him while he did and later, they'd lie on the couch and watch a movie, but they always went to bed together and he made her feel like the most beautiful woman alive. The sex was out of this world. He brought out something in her she'd never known existed with his dominance and power, and she craved his touch.

The words she'd almost said were never mentioned and she understood now why he was reluctant to hear them. He was terrified and that fear wouldn't disappear with her words of love, it would intensify. Mark was trying to control the narrative and she had to let him, for now at least, and keep the status quo.

Her phone ringing on her desk, or at least the conference room desk, flashed with Percy's name and she smiled. She was close to finishing her paper and was itching to get back to her patients and into theatre. Surgery was her life, saving lives her passion, and she missed it like a severed limb.

"Hi, Percy."

"Hello, Savannah. I need you to come into the hospital immediately."

Savannah sat forward, sensing the urgency in his voice that wasn't normally there. Her feet were already moving her towards Mark's office. "What's wrong?"

"It's Melissa Evans. She was just rushed in after a car accident and she's in a bad way."

Savannah instantly switched into doctor mode, her mind shutting out any panic.

"I'm on my way."

"Hurry. It's bad, Savannah, and her mother is frantic."

"Tell her I'll be there shortly."

Savannah hung up as she pushed through Mark's half-open door. His face lit up for a second when he saw her and she never failed to enjoy that look but this wasn't the time to enjoy his carnal looks, her patient needed her.

Mark stood and came around his desk, taking her hands. "What is it?"

"Percy just called me. One of my young patients was in a car accident and I need to go."

Mark frowned. "This could be a trap, doc, I don't like it."

"I don't care, Mark." Savannah stepped back and put her hands on her hips as she glared at him. "This is my job, and Missy is a nineteen-year-old girl just getting her life back. I'll be damned if I'm going to abandon her because I'm scared for my life. My life isn't more important than hers is."

"Okay, calm down. I just meant we need to get security sorted for you. I'd never stop you doing your job, Savannah." His voice was curt now and she regretted being so salty with him. "Let me call Reid and Alex to come with us."

He'd put the desk between them as a barrier and she hated that she'd done that to them. "I'm sorry. It's just I've been seeing Missy since she was a young child. She's finally living her life how she should be, and this happens. I have to fix it."

"I get that, and you will."

In under two minutes, Mark had Reid, Alex, and her in a car on the way to the hospital and she was going over every detail she knew about Missy and her conditions and surgeries and how bad it could be as Reid drove.

Her focus was completely on what she might expect when she walked into that exam room as a troubled Percy met them at the door. Mark kept a few steps back giving her privacy, as he knew patient confidentiality was sacred to her.

"How is she, Percy?"

He clasped her elbow and steered her toward the second floor where her office and the theatres were.

"They took her up already. You need to speak to her parents before you go to theatre. I put them in your office."

Percy knew that she always took the time to check in if she could, and it sounded like she had the few minutes to reassure her mother that she was in good hands. "Thanks, Perc. It isn't her parents though. Her mum is a single mother."

He looked flustered but after the few weeks he'd had, it was hardly a surprise.

Mark grabbed her arm before she walked into her office. "Reid and Alex are checking the theatre, and I need to do a quick check of your office before you go inside."

Savannah waved him on, impatient with the need for this but knowing it was quicker to agree than argue with him. Mark went in and cleared the room, while she waited for his go-ahead.

"It's clear. Stay here for a second. I need to check something with Alex."

"Fine but be quick. I need to head into surgery."

Mark nodded and walked away quickly toward the lift. He nodded and she stepped inside her office. Once inside she discovered the room was empty. Savannah frowned. "Where is Mrs Evans?" she asked Percy.

"Sorry. I must have put them in my office."

Savannah sighed, knowing she'd have to break Mark's rule but not having time to wait. Pulling open the door, she left her office with a glance to the lift. Percy had the office next door. She pushed open the door and strode in with Percy behind her and stopped dead.

The men who had murdered Andy were there and pointing a gun at Mrs Evans and her father. She spun to Percy in shock at his betrayal. "Percy?"

He looked grey now, sweating, and full of shame. "I'm sorry. They have my family. I had no choice." He was openly weeping now as a stoic Mrs Evans sat silently with her elderly father beside her.

"It's okay, Percy."

"Shut the fuck up." The man who'd pulled the trigger spoke, and he seemed to be in charge. He was tall, bald, with thickly corded muscles, and pale blue eyes that had haunted her nightmares for weeks. The other man was shorter and lean, with a nervous, wiry edge about him.

Savannah kept her hands up, knowing she needed to keep her head to get them out of this. Her heart was hammering hard and her hands, normally so steady, shook as she tried to get a handle on her emotions and keep a clear head. "Just let them go and we can talk."

The taller man sneered as he glanced at his friend, waving his gun at her. "Hear that, Tank? She thinks she's in control here."

A pop sounded and Percy gasped as he fell forward clutching his chest, red blood blooming across his white shirt and surprised eyes finding hers as he fell into her, grabbing on for life.

"No!" Savannah went to help her friend, falling on her knees.

"Leave him."

Savannah put her hands over the wound but knew it was helpless. Pain ricocheted through her scalp as a hand grabbed her by her hair and yanked her up, the roots tearing from her head. Covering his hand with her own to ease the burn, she stood and let him throw her across the desk.

"Now, let me explain how this is going to go. You and I are leaving this hospital together. If you come quietly then Mrs Evans and her father here will be back home with little Melissa by dinner time. If not, then Tank will kill them, and it will be your fault."

"You won't get away with this, security will stop you."

"Ah yes, your little guard dogs. You'd better convince them all is well then, or you know what happens. Now let's go so we can talk about this little recording you have. Most inconvenient of you to poke your nose in, doc."

A knock on the door had her tensing.

"Savannah?"

She could hear the concern in Mark's voice as he called her name looking for her. The man was carrying enough guilt without her dying too.

"Tell him everything is fine, and you need him to check the surgical floor."

"He'll want to see me."

"Fine. Crack the door but don't do anything stupid." Tank and Mr No Name shoved their guns at Mrs Evans and her father. Mrs Evans glared but remained silent as she gripped her father's hand.

Savannah took a breath and cracked the door, pasting a smile on her face. "Decker, I'm in Percy's office."

"Oh, thank God. You scared me."

She saw his handsome face come into view and then the relief erode when he noticed the blood on her shirt and the desperate look on her face as she signalled with her eyes.

"Sorry, I was just speaking to Mrs Evans. Can you check the surgical floor for me? I think I have two patients not one, and one has already died."

He glanced at the door and held up two fingers indicating he'd heard her message. "Yeah, but I really should escort you up."

Savannah was thankful he was playing along. "It's fine, Deck. I have two porters that can escort me to the floor."

"Fine. If you're sure?"

"I am."

"Okay, doc. See you there."

Savannah dipped her head and wondered if this was the last conversation she'd get to have with the man she loved and couldn't let herself believe it was. Even if it didn't work out with them, this wasn't how their story ended.

Chapter Twenty

D ecker cursed as he stepped out onto the third floor, something niggling at him about Percy's behaviour. But he couldn't get a signal on his phone and had to go up to the cafeteria where he knew his phone worked.

"Lopez, it's me. I need you to get into the hospital security feed and find out if either of the men we're looking for has been seen in the hospital or near it."

"We have facial rec running to alert us if they do."

"I know but I have a bad feeling about this. Percy was acting weird."

Lopez chuckled. "He *is* fucking weird, that's why."

"Yeah, maybe, also check and see if a Melissa Evans has been booked into the emergency room system."

"Okay, will do."

"Text me the info. I left Savannah in her office alone and don't want to be gone long but I have a shit signal in this place."

He hung up and rushed back down the single flight of stairs to the second floor. He hated leaving Savannah alone for even a second, but he wondered if that was more about his growing attraction to her.

The time they'd spent together this last week had been some of the happiest he could remember and knowing it would end, even though it was the right thing, sucked.

Hitting the second floor, he marched to her office, a sudden sense of urgency filling him. A tension that was invisible swirled around him as the hairs on his neck rose. He went into her office without knocking expecting to see her talking to the patient's family and found it empty.

He called her name as he checked her bathroom and panic began to knot in his belly. Clenching his jaw, he took a breath as he hit the hallway and cleared the room to the left. The silence, something he usually loved, suddenly seemed deafening, and he realised that none of the usual admin staff were on the floor.

His awareness in full flight he hit the alarm on his watch which would tell the team he needed them. He then sent a text to them saying to come in quiet as he had no intel yet. He reached Percy's office and the door opened, her beautiful face in the doorway making relief score through him but the blood on her hands registered before she could hide them in her pockets, and she called him Decker, something she never did.

He was always Mark to her. It had grated initially as only Susie had called him Mark but hearing Savannah say his name soothed his soul in a way he hadn't known he needed until she did it. Now he loved that she called him by his given name. Deciding to play along with whatever she was doing and trusting her, he acted as he would've done if he hadn't seen the blood.

"Oh, thank God. You scared me." He took in the blood on her shirt and the desperate look on her face as she signalled with her eyes that something was very wrong, and she wasn't alone in that room.

"Sorry, I was just speaking to Mrs Evans. Can you check the surgical floor for me? I think I have two patients not one, and one has already died."

Was she trying to tell him there were two other hostages and one dead? He glanced at the door and held up two fingers indicating he'd heard her message and saw the relief on her face and knew he was right.

"Yeah, but I really should escort you up." He was playing along, knowing he wouldn't give up normally and leave her and making it seem more real for whoever was in the room with her. He had a pretty good idea, but either way, they'd either die today or leave in cuffs because they had messed with someone he cared about. He could admit he cared about her, loved her even but he couldn't cope with her loving him.

"It's fine, Deck. I have two porters that can escort me to the floor."

Deck figured she was telling him there were two targets inside. "Fine. If you're sure?"

"I am."

"Okay, doc. See you there."

He watched as she closed the door and retreated to the stairwell where Reid and Alex were waiting.

Reid looked annoyed. "What the fuck is going on? There's no one by the name Melissa Evans here."

"It was a trap. Savannah is in Percy's office with two targets and two hostages. I don't know if that includes her or not, but they also have one dead."

Alex ran his hand through his hair. "I'll have Jack set a perimeter and clear this floor and the one below. They'll want an exit so will need to go down unless they use the roof."

Reid looked toward the roof. "If this is Cavendish, they might send a chopper."

"Have them clear the first floor and roof. Alex and Reid, can you clear this floor? It's like a ghost town out there so I think it's already clear. I don't know why I didn't pick up on it before." Guilt assailed him at the mistake that could cost him everything.

"I'll have Mitch set up across the road in case he can get a shot through the window." Alex was already walking away.

"Hey, don't second guess this, it won't help you."

Reid clapped him on the shoulder and jogged away to clear the floor as he took up position watching the office door. He needed her safe, and away from this madness.

Five minutes that seemed like hours later, Jack strode towards him and instantly took command of the situation. He was dressed for war in tactical gear and weapons and handed him a rifle and ammunition to add to his sidearm which he always carried and a comms earpiece.

"Deck," he said by way of greeting. "Mitch is across the road setting up, but he has eyes on the room. Gunner is in the room above getting us a visual. The cameras in the office are disabled but we think they'll make a break for the roof."

Decker took off his suit jacket and vest and pulled the tactical vest over his head, wrapping the Velcro tight before he rolled his sleeves out of the way and pushed the comms into his ear. He instantly felt grounded as the mission became laser-focused and the woman he cared about was forced into the background. It was the only way he'd keep his head right now.

"How many?"

Jack held up a screen as Gunner pushed the tiny camera through the ceiling and he got a visual of what they were dealing with. There was no audio, but he could see Percy was dead and the two men who'd killed Andy Farr were holding Savannah and two others, a man and woman, hostage. The two men were arguing between themselves as Savannah watched, seeming calm and collected on the surface, even though he knew it would be terrifying for her.

She was the bravest person he knew and so strong and confident. It was such a turn on, but it was her kind heart that brought him to his knees. She was like the sun, and he couldn't seem to get enough, yet he needed it to be enough so he could walk away. In another life, he knew she would've been the woman he spent his life with, but it wasn't, and that ship had sailed when he'd laid his wife and son in the ground.

"Reid and Waggs are covering the roof in case they try for that." Jack tapped his earpiece. *"Mitch, do you have a shot?"*

"Affirmative, I have a shot on the smaller target nearest the window."

Jack turned to Decker. "Our best option is a full assault. We breech the door as Mitch takes out the one near the window and we take the other man down. If we wait, the chances are we'll lose more hostages and we both know they won't negotiate. Carter would have them tortured and killed if they surrender."

"What about crossfire?"

Jack angled his head. "Now isn't the time for doubt, Deck. We've practised this very drill a hundred times, and we've never hit an innocent."

"This is different."

"No, it isn't. It can't be because that's how mistakes happen. Can you handle this, or shall I pull Reid from the roof?"

Jack wasn't being a dick, Decker knew that, but he still bristled at the warning tone. "I can handle it."

"Good" Jack tapped his earpiece again. *"Gunner, continue the live feed. Listen up all call signs, we're going to breach as soon as Mitch takes out the first man."*

Alex and Blake joined them and ducking low, moved to cover the two doors that lead from the floor and disabled the lift. The last thing they needed was anyone getting in or out.

Alex nodded and Deck and Jack crept across the floor and stood on either side of the door to Percy's office. They could hear arguing inside and Jack used the sound to fit a small device to the hinge to blow the door enough for it to open when kicked.

"Hostages one and two are seated in chairs to the right of the desk and target one now has hostage three in a chokehold with her body as a shield. He's arguing with the larger hostile." Gunner relayed the information giving them a picture of what was happening.

"Mitch do you still have a shot?"

"Affirmative."

Jack looked at him as if waiting for his go ahead and he took a breath. If Savannah was the hostage in the man's hold, the slightest

141

mistake by Mitch and she'd be dead, but he also trusted his team and Mitch was the best. He didn't make mistakes and had sounded confident.

He gave the nod and the next thing he knew Jack was giving the order to execute. As the door blew out, Decker aimed and fired at the man who'd turned towards them looking bewildered and trusted Mitch to make the shot. With two shots to the body and one to the head the man fell, his body landing on Percy behind the desk and the smaller man fell forward, a hole between his eyes from Mitch's bullet. Savannah stumbled and then he was holding her while the rest of the team streamed in and checked the other hostages over.

He ran his hands all over her body, cupping her face in his hands as she clung to him. "Are you hurt?"

"No."

He could see she was lying but he let it go knowing she'd deny it and that whatever it was wasn't serious or she would've said.

She turned toward the man who'd been her boss and friend and he felt the moment the magnitude of this hit her and she collapsed against him. "Percy is dead."

"It's okay, doc. I have you. It's going to be okay. I promise." He held her to his body as he guided her out of the room and into her own office which was quiet. He motioned to Jack as he went so he knew where he was.

He sank down beside her and held her in his arms as she curled into his body, making herself small. He realised at that moment that he loved her, that she was his world and he wanted to give her everything but had nothing to give her except her freedom. As soon as she was safe, he'd do just that. The thought made him feel sick as he pressed his lips to her head. A life without her loomed, but she deserved so much better than him. Her hand gripped his shirt as he stroked her hair gently. He inhaled her scent and knew his time with her was short. Shadow was already working on a deal with the two older Cavendish brothers, and it wouldn't be long before she was free to live her life and find a man worthy of her and have the family she deserved.

Not with a man who'd already let one family down so badly, resulting in their deaths, and one determined not to do the same again. His job was the only thing that was safe, it kept him grounded and he could not guarantee he wouldn't fuck it up and put her behind Eidolon and make the same mistakes again. He'd loved Susie, would always love her but what he felt for the woman in his arms eclipsed even that. He wouldn't watch this incredible woman, who he knew had so much to give, play second fiddle to his job, and he couldn't make promises he wouldn't be able to keep.

Chapter Twenty-One

The entire Eidolon team had turned out for Percy's funeral, which was held at his local church. Mark had stood beside her the entire time, his hand always touching her in some way. Holding her hand or with light pressure at the small of her back, just so she knew he was there, and she'd needed it. What happened to Andy was sad, but Percy's death was tragic. He'd been an innocent and now his husband would raise their two daughters alone.

Her heart had felt heavy since the funeral but that wasn't all that was on her mind. Mark was pulling away; she could feel his emotional distance like a physical loss. He still cooked for her, and he made love to her every night, and it was tender and passionate and still had that sexy edge of dominance she loved. He kissed her like she was the only person in his life who mattered.

It was subtle changes; like he didn't hold her all night as he had before. He also made sure he was up before her every morning and dressed so they no longer shared a shower. He had lunch with one of his teammates instead of her, and more importantly, he couldn't seem to look her in the eye.

Closing the romantic comedy novel she was reading, she laid it on the couch. Mark was in his home office working as he did most evenings and she felt edgy and unsettled. Like she needed to run or do something to get rid of these feelings of panic.

Blake and Gunner were outside today, and she knew they were far from convinced about her safety, hence why she was still living here. The truth was she didn't want to leave but she knew the time was coming.

She needed to get out of her head and maybe using the home gym Mark had set up would help. She could do no more with the hospital until the board made a decision about a new head. Her eyes pricked with tears at the thought of Percy and his grieving family. Wiping the lone tear away, she opened her eyes wide to try and make herself look happier and went to find Mark.

She knocked on the door and poked her head in to find him on the phone. She made to back away, but he motioned her inside with a smile that made her insides melt. What was it about this man that made her turn to mush? *Oh, that's right, he's sexy, kind, thoughtful, looked like a god, fucked like the devil, and she loved being with him.*

Moving into the room she leaned against the windowsill and listened.

"Are you sure, Jack? I won't have her at risk." His eyes were on her as he nodded at whatever Jack was saying.

"Okay, that's good enough for me. I'll let her know and thank Shadow for me."

Savannah had no idea who Shadow was, and she'd heard the term often, but she also knew not to ask questions. There was more to Eidolon than she'd first realised, and she figured sometimes less was more. Mark hung up the phone and looked up at her with a wide smile, his shoulders seeming to slump in relief.

"Everything all right?"

He stood and crossed to her, his hands landing on her hips and bringing her tight against him. Instantly her body began to hum with desire. He lifted her and set her on his desk as he stepped between her thighs, spreading them wide. "Everything is great. Shadow has made a deal with the Cavendish brothers to secure your safety. I don't know the details, nor do I need to, but they've guaranteed you're safe from them and Carter."

His hands wandered over her skin, touching her everywhere as Savannah ran her hands over his flexing biceps. She loved how strong he was, how beautiful his body was, he made her feel cherished and small. "Really? So, I can go back to surgery?"

Mark laughed as he threw his head back exposing the thick column of his neck and it was a wonderful sound after all the silence. "I should've guessed that would be your first thought." He kissed her neck as he pushed her oversized shirt off her shoulder. "Yes, you can go back to surgery."

His lips grew more frantic on her skin as she arched against him, giving him more room. She could sense the urgency in him, felt the air change as the dominant sexual being overtook him. She loved him when he could hardly keep it together. When he was frantic to be inside her.

"I want you to fuck me on your desk." Her hands pulled at his clothes, desperate to feel his warm skin under her fingers. He tore at her shirt, sending buttons flying and unhooking her bra, letting it fall to the floor.

With his hand between her breasts, he pushed her back on his desk and surveyed her. Goosebumps broke out all over her body at the heated gaze filled with possession. "Fuck me, you're beautiful."

Her body ached to feel him inside her, every nerve strung so tight she thought she might climax from just his kiss. He played her body like a fine violin, knowing each stroke that would give her the most pleasure.

"Mark, I need you." Her hands were at his hips, grasping wildly at his zipper before she finally freed his hard cock. She stroked him twice just how he liked it, watching his eyes turn to onyx before he threw his head back in pleasure.

"That feels so fucking good, but I need to be inside that tight pussy."

Savannah loved his filthy mouth when they had sex. He was so prim and buttoned up most of the time and she loved that she got to see that side of him.

He pulled away from her touch and quickly dragged her leggings and panties down her legs. He was still partially dressed and that added to the arousal running through her. She was so exposed, and he looked uncontrolled and wild.

"Mark." She reached for him, and he bent to kiss her, his tongue sliding through her mouth as his cock rubbed through her soaked sex. Her legs clamped around his waist, and he was inside her, his hard dick stretching her as he pushed in to the base. Her body clenched around him, and he shuddered, his entire body moving beneath her hands.

"So tight and wet. Fuck. You slay me, doc."

"Fuck me."

His head lifted and he gave her a sexy smile. "Such a dirty mouth for a professional woman."

She had no answer because he pulled out and slammed into her, giving her exactly what she begged for. He groaned with each hard stroke of his hips, her body slid across the desk, he was fucking her hard, and she loved it. He laced his fingers with hers and thrust their joined hands above her head on the desk. His lips dipped and pulled her tight nipple into his mouth.

Her body was alive, every cell zinging with electricity, and she whimpered in pleasure, in fear. This was so much more than anything they had shared before and she was scared this climax would send her over the edge.

"It's okay, doc, let go. I've got you. I want to feel you come all over my cock."

His words were like a trigger, and she came so hard her world exploded in flashing colour, every muscle clenched, and she heard Mark moan loudly as he pumped his hips and his orgasm hit with a roar.

Her legs slumped to the side as he fell onto her, kissing her neck as her hands stroked the silky strands of his hair. She loved the sex, but this moment right here was her perfection. When they were both satiated and she saw the real Mark Decker. He looked at her and smiled and said the words that were in her heart.

"I love you, Mark."

His face fell and she instantly regretted her impulsive words as he pulled away from her and they were both confronted with the realisation they'd just had sex without a condom.

"Fuck, that was a mistake."

He looked angry and scared, and she wanted to reassure him.

Savannah sat up on the desk, suddenly feeling exposed and vulnerable which he'd never made her feel before. "It's okay, I'm on the pill."

He looked at her with disdain and hatred and she felt her heart shrivel in pain. "It is not okay, Savannah."

He stalked away to the bathroom, leaving her feeling cheap and unsure. She stood and straightened her clothes as she listened to him in the bathroom. Dressed, she felt marginally more prepared for the storm she knew was coming. She should have waited to tell him she loved him.

When he walked back in, his armour was back in place. His three-piece suit, shirt, and perfectly knotted tie made him look untouchable.

"Can we talk?" she asked, standing to go to him and stopping as he gave her a look that would put the fear of God in any man. She wasn't afraid of him, he'd never physically hurt her, but he had the power to do so much worse.

"No, there's nothing to talk about. You're safe and this arrangement is over."

"Mark, please."

"No, Savannah." He swiped his hand through the air with finality. "We had fun, but this was never more. I'm sorry you let your feelings get involved but I don't love you. I love my wife and, I'm sorry to say, you would be a poor substitute for her, a cheap copy."

If he'd struck her, he couldn't have hurt her more. She felt like her insides were collapsing, her heart tearing open, and she wondered how she was still alive. Tears ran freely down her cheeks now. She knew exactly what he was doing, and to some extent, she understood but she had to make him see reason. "Mark, don't do this to us, to me."

He straightened his cuffs and looked at her as if she were an irritant. "I'm not doing anything. There is no us."

She knew he was lying, could see it in his eyes, no man touched a woman like he did her if he felt nothing. "You're lying, you care for me. I could feel it when you touched me."

"That was merely a physical response to a good fuck."

"Why are you doing this?" She couldn't stop the sobs now, no matter how hard she tried to save her dignity.

"Stop the waterworks, Savannah, it won't work. It's time for you to leave."

"You want me to go right now?"

He folded his arms, and she could feel her heartbreak turn to fury. How dare he treat her this way.

"I think it's best."

Savannah walked to the door, his scent almost crushing her as she walked past him. She stopped at the door and turned back to him as he sat behind his desk and opened his laptop as if he hadn't just broken her heart. "If I walk out that door, there is no going back."

He met her eyes and his were cold as he nodded. "Very well." He dropped his eyes back to the screen. "Close the door on your way out."

Savannah left it open in a petulant sign of rebellion and ran upstairs. She packed her things, shoving them in a bag, eager to get out of there before she broke down uncontrollably and begged him. She loved him and knew this was his stupid way of protecting himself, but she wouldn't be his whipping boy. He needed to find his own way and if what they'd had the last few weeks wasn't enough, he'd die a lonely old man. Zipping the bag, she took one last glance around the room and left. She walked down the stairs and past his office which now had the door closed and out the front door.

Gunner saw the look on her face and rushed to her, worry etched on his handsome face.

He looked back to the house as her legs gave way. "Savannah, what is it?"

"Nothing. Can you give me a ride home?"

His arm came around her and she saw him frown at Blake and nod toward the house. "Find out what the hell happened."

He turned back to her. "Yes, of course. Would you like me to call Lacey?"

He was such a sweet man and Lacey was so lucky, but she needed to be alone and with her own things right now. She shook her head. "No. Just take me home please."

He guided her to his car and helped her in as if she'd break. As she looked back at the house and saw the man she loved standing in the window watching her leave, she thought she might too.

Chapter Twenty-Two

"Get dressed, asshole, we're going out." Gunner threw clothes at him as he sat on the couch nursing a hangover from hell. He remembered now why he'd given up drinking, it made him feel like shit and the pain was still there when he woke up.

He glanced at Gunner who was still pissed at him for the way he'd treated Savannah. "Not in the mood."

"I don't give a fuck. You're getting your ass out of this house and coming out with the boys."

"Why? So you can all tell me what a dick I am again?"

His friends hadn't pulled their punches when they'd found out what he'd done, and it was his own stupid fault. Savannah hadn't said a word, it was his own drunken ramblings that had revealed that stellar moment.

Savannah. Just the thought of her made his heart ache with loss. He fucking missed her so much. Her laugh, her touch, the way she made him feel, the way she held him to account, never letting him get away with his shit but not holding a grudge either. She was the best person he knew, and he'd thrown it all away.

He'd never known love like this before. He'd loved his wife and had been happy with her, but this was more, deeper. What he felt for Susie was sweet and gentle, with Savannah it was rip-your-heart-out passion.

"You're a dick. How anyone could treat a woman like her that way is a fucking crime. But it's done and a month is long enough for you to wallow. You made your choice, now man the fuck up and live with it."

A t-shirt landed on his head as Gunner threw it and then stood over him with his hands on his hips. This wasn't a fight he was going to win so he stood and glared at his friend. He knew deep down the tough love was something he would've given him if the reverse were happening, and he'd treated Lacey the way he had Savannah.

"And take a fucking shower. You stink."

Decker flipped him the bird but did indeed take a shower and felt human for the first time in weeks. He'd been working but other than that he was surviving. He met Gunner at the door and locked up before pointing at his car. "I'll drive. I think staying sober is a good plan."

"Fine." Gunner folded his huge body into the car, his mood still not great but mellowing.

"Where to?"

"The Imperial."

Decker parked down the road and they walked into the bar ten minutes later. He glanced around for his friends and found them at the bar. Jack waved them over where they had taken over most of the corner.

"Good to see you're alive. What you drinking?"

"I'll have a sparkling water, please."

Jack got Gunner's order and then turned to the barmaid who was practically salivating at him and got a round in.

Liam came over and grabbed his shoulders. "Deck, did you hear the news?"

"No, what'd I miss?"

"I'm gonna be a daddy!"

The joy on Liam's face could be seen from space and Decker was genuinely happy for him.

He slapped him on the back as he hugged him. "Congratulations, man, I'm so happy for you both. You're gonna be great parents."

"Thanks, man, I'm so excited."

"It's the best feeling in the world," he admitted and glanced across the room, his eyes locking with the woman he loved and had thrown away. She was sitting at a table with all the women and as soon as she saw him, she looked away as if he meant nothing to her. It stung more than he could've imagined and the ache for her in his belly knotted tight.

"Sorry, Deck, I didn't know she'd be here," Gunner said from beside him as he noticed him stiffen.

Decker shook it off, he'd done this to himself and had nobody to blame for his pain except himself. "It's fine." He turned to Blake. "Blake, how is fatherhood treating you?"

Blake beamed despite the bags under his eyes from his two-week-old daughter Ariella keeping him awake. "Best feeling in the world. I never knew I could feel such love for another human."

"Shit. Don't let Pax hear you say that. She'll have your balls." Jack laughed as he glanced across at his wife and winked. Those two wouldn't be far behind on this baby train, the love between them was palpable.

"Nah, it's different and she'd agree. I adore Pax and she knows it but the love you have for your child is beyond explaining."

Decker did know, he'd felt it every day since Milo and his daughter were conceived. He glanced back at Savannah and frowned not seeing her. His eyes scanned the room looking for her, panic seizing him before he found her further down the bar. His jaw clenched as anger assailed him when he saw some drunk douchebag was standing too close beside her and chatting her up.

His gut churned when she laughed at something he said and then they both laughed. Was she on a date? Had she moved on so quickly from what they'd shared? Jealousy clouded his vision and before he knew it, he was walking over to them.

He saw her face drain of colour when she saw him and that pissed him off more. She'd never had a need to be afraid of him. "Savannah."

"Hello, Mark." Her voice was like music to his ears after an entire twenty-eight days without hearing it. Soft and melodic but with a confidence that made his dick hard.

"Who's your friend?" He gripped his glass harder as the dickhead tried to elbow him out of the way.

"Buzz off, buddy. This one is mine."

Decker gave the man a stony cold stare as he tried to claim Savannah. "I think you'll find she isn't."

The man turned to him fully and his eyes were unfocused as he tried to stare him down. He almost felt sorry for the man who was way out of Savannah's league.

"Oh, for God's, sake." Savannah threw up her hands. "I'm not a fucking bone to fight over. I don't belong to anyone," she turned to him with fire in her eyes, "least of all you."

With that, she spun on her heel and walked out the door.

"Savannah," he called but she kept walking.

Mark brushed past the man and followed her, not wanting this interaction to end, and having no clue what he'd say. He caught up with her as she crossed the car park and grabbed her arm, spinning her to face him.

"For fucks sake, wait up, Savannah."

She yanked her arm from his grip and stepped back. "Don't fucking touch me."

She was furious and much as it made him a dick, it turned him on to see so much fire in her. It was one of the things he loved about her. The air practically danced with the electricity between them as her breathing heaved and he fought for control.

"How dare you think you can come up to me and scare some man who was just talking to me. Who the hell do you think you are?

You don't want me, but you don't want anyone else to have me, is that it?"

Deck could see the pain he was causing her, had caused her, and regretted every single tear she'd shed for him. Hurting her was one of his biggest regrets and he'd do anything to take it back. "I do want you, Savannah."

He moved toward her, his hands reaching for her as the words left him in a broken admission. In the next second, she was in his arms, and he was kissing like she was the air he needed to breathe. He tried to tell how he felt with his body as he crushed her to him, need throbbing through him. God, he'd missed her.

Suddenly she broke from his arms on a sob. "No." Her swollen lips taunted him but the hurt in her eyes was worse. "What's changed, Mark?"

He looked at her with an apology in his eyes and saw her anguish and wondered if his face reflected the same. "I'm sorry, doc."

"You don't want anyone else playing with your toy is that it?"

"No, of course not. I do want you. I want you so bad. I miss you, but I can't give you what you need, Savannah."

"Bullshit." She folded her arms across her middle as if trying to stop him from inflicting more pain. "You don't know what I need because you never asked. But you got one thing right, I'm too good for you. I deserve a man who loves me enough to be brave."

She turned on her heel and ran to her car and he watched her go, wondering how much more he could take and why he felt like he'd just let his salvation walk out of his life.

With heavy feet, he wandered back into the bar where every one of his teammates was now with the women they loved. He saw the love and laughter, the shared joy and excitement between the couples and knew he needed to get away and get his head straight. He couldn't keep on living this half-life, and to move on and have a future like the one he desperately wanted with Savannah he needed to let the past go.

"Jack, do you have a minute?"

Jack stood and kissed his wife with a grin before he made his way over to him. "What's up?"

"I need some time off."

"Okay, no problem. How much?"

"Not sure yet. I need to get my head straight and face a few demons and maybe say goodbye to some things."

"This about Savannah?"

"In part, but I also need to do this for me."

Jack gripped his shoulder. "Take all the time you need, but we're here if you need us. We aren't just friends, we're your family."

"I know and I appreciate it, but I need to do this alone."

"Fair enough but stay in touch. If we think you need us, we'll be there anyway, understand?"

"Thanks, Jack."

"No problem."

"Oh, one last thing. Can you keep an eye on Savannah for me? She's upset and I hate the thought of her being alone."

Jack smiled a knowing grin and nodded. "I'll have Astrid handle it."

Decker walked out of the pub, went home, packed a bag, and headed for the airport. It was time to confront his past.

Chapter Twenty-Three

D ecker looked up into the mirror behind the bar where he was nursing an untouched glass of bourbon. It had been two weeks since he'd packed his bags and flown home to the States, except it didn't feel like home anymore. He'd visited his parents briefly, which had been a disaster as they lamented him for not visiting more. He understood it, they missed him but the way they were was part of the reason he'd stayed away.

After Susie and Milo had died, they'd been heartbroken. When Susie's family had lashed out at him for taking her away from them and moving her to New York, blaming him for their deaths, they'd taken their side. He understood it was said in grief and had never held it against them, but it was why he'd stayed away.

"Drinking alone is for losers."

Decker lifted his head and smiled in surprise seeing the face of his friend Scott Silverman. They'd been in the FBI together and now Scott was on an FBI serial killer task force in Texas.

He shook his friend's hand and gave him a hearty backslap. "Scott, what brings you out here?"

"Oh, ya know, a little birdy told me my friend was here and hadn't bothered to reach out, so I thought I'd come and kick his ass."

"Drink?"

"Sure, whatever you're drinking."

"Well, I was nursing a bourbon but haven't got the stomach for it, so how about a beer?"

"Sounds good." Scott slid onto the stool next to him as Decker motioned to the bartender for two beers.

Taking the beer, he took a sip and sighed as it hit the spot. "I guess Jack sent you?"

"They became a little concerned when they didn't hear from you."

"I sent them a text to let them know I was okay."

"Maybe but you know how a team as tight as yours is, they care. I know if I did the same, Condor and Hawk would be banging my door down."

Decker sighed and looked at the man he hardly recognised in the mirror. He'd stopped wearing his suits since arriving, trying to shed the armour he'd thought had kept him safe and untouchable. "I know. I should've called."

"What's going on, Deck?"

He hadn't stopped thinking about Savannah these last weeks, but Susie was on his mind a lot now too. What would she think about him moving on? Did she blame him? And why were his feelings Savannah so much more real? "I met a woman."

"That's great. About damn time."

"I fucked it all up."

"Ah, I see." Scott took a drink and placed his glass on the bar. "Want to talk about it?"

"No point, I can't fix it."

"Have you tried?"

Decker swung towards his friend, his hand swiping through his hair in frustration. "Why? I have nothing to offer her."

"Tell me about her."

Scott was always so calm, so focused. It was no wonder he was such a good agent and had bagged himself a wonderful wife.

"She's a neurosurgeon, top in her field and beautiful too. She has these big hazel eyes and dimples in her cheeks when she smiles, and she's always smiling. God, it lights up the room with its brilliance. And she's kind and so damn funny. She can't cook for shit but makes a mean sandwich and buys these little cupcakes that she can decorate herself."

"She sounds amazing. What's the issue?"

"She loves me."

Scott snorted into his beer. "Sorry, what? She loves you? I take it you don't feel the same. Although this day drinking in a shithole bar suggests otherwise."

"No, I do love her."

Scott laid his hands on his knees and looked at him sideways like he was crazy and maybe he was. "So, she loves you and you love her. What exactly is the problem?"

"I loved Susie too and I couldn't protect her. What if it happens again? I can't go through that again, Scott. You saw me."

"Jeez, Decker." He could hear the sympathy in his friend's voice and hated he was the beneficiary of it. "That accident wasn't your fault. It was nobody's fault. The driver had a heart attack at the wheel. It was a tragic accident. If you'd been there, it still would've happened and likely with the same outcome. You know that."

"I need someone to blame."

"I know and for ten years it's been yourself but now it's time to honour your wife and son and live a life they never got the chance to."

"What if it happens again? She's the only person who makes me feel whole."

"Listen, Deck. I know it must be terrifying for you and I can't imagine what you went through and don't even want to try but loving someone is a risk. It's the payoff for the beauty we have with them.

We can't live with fear, or we aren't living, and I hate to tell you but it's too late."

"Meaning?"

Scott stood. "If you love her the risk is already in play. Not being with her won't ease that pain if something happens to her, it will make you regret every second you wasted."

Scott's words were like a slap in the face and the reality of them hit him hard. He was right, not being with her wouldn't ease the loss if something bad happened, it would make it worse. Had he made a terrible mistake?

"Come on, let's get out of here and grab some food." Scott threw some bills on the bar and Decker followed him in a daze as he drove them to a diner close by.

"I see what I said is sinking in."

Decker tucked into some eggs and bacon, deep in thought. "Yeah, I guess it is."

"You need to let the past go and get your ass on a plane and fix this."

His appetite was suddenly back with gusto, and Decker smiled for the first time since he'd broken the heart of the woman he loved. "Yeah, I do, and believe me, I have some serious sucking up to do. I was a complete asshole to her."

"How?" Scott frowned.

Decker admitted his hurtful words shame rolling over him as Scott winced. "Ouch. Good luck."

"I know. I deserve whatever she dishes out, but I won't give up. She brought me back to life and I need her to know that. But first I have to say goodbye."

"Sounds like a plan. Penny and I want an invite to the wedding."

"Ha, I have to get her to forgive me first."

"You will."

* * *

He walked up the hill to the cemetery where his family rested and noted the beauty in the colours of the trees fading from green to the vibrant orange of fall. Natures last spectacular display before it slept for the winter. His heart ached as he got closer to the plot where the two graves lay side by side.

Decker had made peace with his and Susie's parents, and while they may never understand his actions, they didn't blame him anymore for the deaths of their daughter and grandson. It had been grief in all its heart-breaking glory that had caused them to lash out.

He stopped and ran his hand over the headstone, knocking several fallen leaves to the ground, the names of the people he loved etched in the smooth stone. Kneeling, he cleared away the flowers he knew his in-laws laid weekly and placed a bouquet of her favourite daisies in their place.

"Hey, Susie, sorry I haven't been in a while. You know I was never one for believing that you were here. I didn't need to visit. I feel you with me everywhere I go." His hand rested on his heart as his eyes stung with tears as he tried to find the words.

"I met someone. I know you always said if anything happened to you to move on and find love and it's taken me ten years, but I've found her. She's wonderful, kind, clever, beautiful inside and out, and she doesn't take any shit from me. I tried not to love her. I was so scared. Losing you and Milo broke me and I never thought I'd heal from it, but she put me back together without me even realising it. I guess it's a good thing she's a doctor."

He chuckled at his own thoughts but fell sombre. "I need you to know that I'll always love you and miss you until the day I die but it's time for me to love another now, and I do. I love her so much and I hope you understand that it takes nothing away from what we had. I was lucky enough to have two soul mates in my life. You were my first and she'll be my last."

His eyes drifted over his son's name and that brought pain of a different kind, a deeper loss than he could even comprehend. "I know Milo is with you, and you're together. Tell him I love him and miss his Lego creations but that I'll see him one day, and until then I'll keep all three of you in a safe place in my heart."

He wished he could have a sign from her that it was okay, that she forgave him, but he knew that was nonsense. He stood and kissed his fingers before dropping them to the headstone. "I love you both so much," his voice cracked on the last word, and he blinked as two robins landed on the headstone.

His face cracked into a smile as he looked heavenward. "Thanks, Susie."

He watched the birds fly away and then turned to head back to his car. As he did his footsteps stalled. Leaning against a black SUV, were his teammates. He guessed Scott must have called them.

He jogged closer to the four men, Waggs, Reid, Jack, and Gunner, who looked calm as they waited for him.

"What are you guys doing here? Is everything okay?"

Jack took off his sunglasses despite the glare of the fall sun and smiled. "We've come to take you home. It's time."

"And you flew halfway around the world for that?"

Gunner stepped forward and slung his arm around him. "You've saved each one of us in one way or another and now it's time for us to step up for you."

Decker looked at them. "I did my job."

Waggs chuckled. "No, Decker, you were a friend. You always protect us and now we want you to know we have your back. Yes, we were hard on you over Savannah but that's because we care about you, and we saw how good she was for you." Reid laughed. "Plus, I got to visit my mom and sisters while we were here."

Gunner joined in. "Yeah, and Mrs Reid is an awesome cook."

"How long have you been here?"

"Three days."

"And you stayed away?" He was surprised to say the least.

"You needed time and now you need to get your ass on the company jet and fix your cock-up." Jack opened the car door, ever the boss man.

"I need to grab my stuff."

"No need. We got it from your hotel and closed out your bill. Leave the rental, Scott is collecting it for us."

That was Jack, snowballing over people and taking charge like he did best, and this time Decker was happy for it. He was ready to go home and fix his mistakes.

He felt lighter now than he had in years with the forgiveness of his family and the silent blessing he'd had from Susie and felt able to make the last step towards his future—hopefully with Savannah.

As they landed at the private airfield the following day, they were met by Mitch, his face stoic and calm as he shook Deck's hand and welcomed him back.

"What's up, Mitch? I can see something isn't right. You don't normally meet us at the airfield."

"Sorry to land this on you as soon as you got back, but we've just had word from Aubrey. The stalker Savannah had, that we thought was Andy Farr, was actually his pregnant girlfriend and now we can't find her or Savannah."

His heart went into freefall as fear slammed into him. *God, not again.*

Chapter Twenty-Four

"I can't believe you didn't tell me before." Addie pursed her lips in annoyance and Savannah dropped her head.

"I'm sorry, Addie, I didn't want to worry you, and honestly, I'm sick of the drama in my life so you must be sick of hearing it."

Addie grabbed her free hand across the table in the hospital coffee shop. "Sav, you're my friend and you were there for me. Let me do the same, okay?"

"Fine, I'll tell you if anything else happens. But Aubrey knows about the break-in at my office and the damage done to my car. I'm sure it's nothing but silly kids having fun."

"Maybe, but we're not taking any risks. I'm telling Lopez to keep an eye on your place."

Savannah smiled for the first time in weeks. "You do realise how creepy that sounds right?"

"I know, but I don't care. You're my best friend and I won't lose you to some nut job."

Savannah grinned as she blew on her hot chocolate. "What about Astrid?"

Addie waved her hand in the air. "She's my sister, she doesn't count."

Savannah laughed. "Okay, but don't let her hear you say that."

Addie joined in and then they sobered. "How are you really doing, Savannah?"

Savannah knew exactly what Addie was asking and wasn't sure how to answer. She'd finally stopped crying herself to sleep and come to terms with the fact she'd foolishly let herself fall in love with a man she couldn't have and who would never want her. He didn't love her and had never lied about that. It had been her own silly fault to think what they had went beyond the rules he'd set. He'd never lied to her or offered her anything more, she'd let her heart get carried away and paid the price.

It was a horrible feeling to know that twice in her life she hadn't been enough for the man she loved but she had to accept it. Andy had been a lost cause from the start and while she thought she'd loved him, and in her own way had, what she felt for Mark almost destroyed her with the loss.

"I'm okay." She shrugged. "I miss him but what we had wasn't real, at least not for him. I was a fool and fell in love with a man who was unavailable. Now I have to move on. Luckily I'm really busy with work."

"I'm so sorry, Savannah, I really thought he loved you. The way he looked at you. God, it made me melt and I have my own hot guy."

"That was lust, not love. They're very different beasts." She couldn't allow her hopes to go wild with Addie's words. That route only led to heartbreak for her, and she was done with all that. "Anyway, it's done. I need to move on. Which brings me to my next bit of news."

"Oh?"

"I've been offered the position as head of Neurosurgery at the Gesundheit Institute in Germany."

Addie blinked in shock. "What? That's amazing, I'm so proud of you." Addie's face dropped. "Does that mean you're leaving?"

"Yes. It's based in Berlin, so I'd have to transfer."

"Are you going to take it?"

Savannah nodded even though the thought of leaving her home and these people made her sad. "Yes, I think so. Apart from you and Astrid and a few friends, I have nothing keeping me here. Percy and Andy are gone. The fate of the neurosurgery department is in doubt with the new board wanting distance from the troubles we've had, and it's my dream job."

"So why don't you look happy about it?"

"I am happy, I just..." She sighed and pushed her cup away. "I guess my goals changed and I have to readjust my mind back to wanting them. I'd imagined this whole life with Mark here with my friends. I know that was stupid when we'd hadn't been together long or rather fucking for long but that's what happened and now, I need to kick my own ass into seizing this opportunity."

"Well, I'll miss you like crazy but if it's what you want you should take it but expect monthly visits from me and Payton and Javier if he can get the time off."

"You'd better visit me, and I'll visit when I can too. It's a great chance to really work with cutting edge techniques that will save hundreds of lives and I can be at the forefront of that and teach others."

"Then I'm excited for you."

"I am too." And she was. For the first time in weeks, she felt excited about her job.

Addie hugged her as they walked out of the coffee shop and went in separate directions. She was about to head up to the second floor when Darla Jenkins walked toward her. Savannah tried not to roll her eyes. She had little time for the woman who'd fucked her husband, but she was grieving the man she'd loved and lost and was now heavily pregnant.

Her fake Botox filled lips curved into a semblance of a smile that wasn't fooling anyone as she laid her hand on her distended stomach. "Hi, Savannah."

"Hello, Darla. How are you?"

"I'm coping, just. Do you have time to help me with something? I have a box in my car, and I can't lift it in my condition. With Andy gone, I have nobody to help me."

The last thing Savannah wanted to do was help this shrew, but her manners won out and there was no way she was watching a pregnant woman struggle. "Sure, lead the way."

Savannah held her hand out to Darla to go first out of the hospital but instead of turning left toward the staff parking, she headed towards the direction of the slip road where delivery drivers pulled in behind the hospital in a loading zone. "Where's your car parked?"

Darla pointed to the slip road. "Oh, I couldn't get a car park earlier, so I left it over there."

"You should really think about parking under the light where it's safe, you know."

As they made it to the furthest point from the hospital to an area concealed by hedge and shrubbery, she glanced around, unease creeping along her neck. She shook it off knowing it was a holdover from everything she'd been through.

"Here we are."

Darla stopped at a silver VW golf and lifted the boot lid, revealing the smallest box she could imagine. She was about to step back and tell Darla off for wasting her time when she felt a prick in her neck and then a shove. She turned, seeing the needle in Darla's hand as her head began to swim, her legs feeling heavy as she tried to form a word and found she couldn't.

Darla leaned forward and pushed her, and she fell into the small boot, her limbs useless and uncooperative.

"It's time we took a drive, Dr Sankey."

Her giggle was terrifying as Savannah blinked and the boot lid went down. She had no idea what Darla had given her, but it was some sort of paralytic that was keeping her conscious but with no use of any function.

She'd never been so scared in her life as the car began to move beneath her. She realised it had been Darla all along with the threats and vandalism. The woman was crazy, and the only hope Savannah had was that someone noticed she was gone, or this damn drug wore off.

Why, oh why, did this keep happening to her? Was she cursed in some way to have all this shit thrown her way? She'd thought she'd led a good life, but she must have been an absolute asshole in a previous one to garner this kind of bad karma.

Her mind was clear and after they had been on the road for about thirty minutes, she began to feel pins and needles in her legs and fingers. Pain assaulted her at the sensation, and she tried not to cry out knowing it was a good thing as it meant her nerves were waking up.

Too soon the car stopped, and she heard Darla get out of the vehicle and the crunch of footsteps on gravel. She had no idea where they were, but she swore she could hear running water over the fear and adrenalin in her ears.

The boot opened and light flooded her eyes making her blink and Darla stood over her with a smirk. "Come on, out you come."

She pulled at Savannah whose limbs were still mostly useless dragging her over the boot lip and letting her fall to the ground on her face. Pain lanced through her cheekbone, and she whimpered, the first sound her vocal cords had allowed.

"For fucks sake, doc? Do I have to do all the work?"

Savannah had no idea what the fuck she wanted her to do but she tried to roll on her back to get away and was rewarded with a swift kick from the deranged woman.

"Don't get clever with me, Savannah. I have a nice trip planned for us and then we're going to go and meet Andy together."

Savannah watched in horror as Darla reached under her top and pulled away a fake baby bump. She must have made a sound because Darla glanced her way before bending down so she was eye level with her. "Yes, now you see. I lost my baby, my precious child gone because of you and now you're going to pay."

Darla spat the last words, venom and hatred evident in every syllable. Her fingers now had movement, and her legs were cramping, and she tried to keep still. She'd need the element of surprise if she was going to get out of this alive. Darla grabbed her by her hair making Savannah cry out in pain as her heavy arms tried to move to ease the pressure on her skull.

"Ah, I see the drug is wearing off. I best hurry before you have the ability to swim." She continued to drag her towards a small boat.

"You know they say drowning is a beautiful way to die and that you have a feeling of euphoria before you go. I want that to be the way I go to meet my Andy and our child. The one who died because you were being such a bitch to my Andy, and it made him end things between us. The stress of it all was too much for my angel and she had to leave us."

Savannah knew the woman was grieving and in a bad way mentally and was convinced this was all Savannah's fault, but she had to try and reason with her. "Darla, I had no idea about the baby." Her voice was weak and scratchy as if unused for months. "I told Andy I didn't want him back and that he needed to make a life with you and the baby."

Darla slammed her body against the boat and cold hatred fell over her with one look. "Get in the boat."

Savannah shook her head. "No, Darla. You don't have to do this. We can fix this." Darla produced a gun from behind her back and Savannah reared back knowing this was going to end with one of them dead. "Please, Darla."

"No, perfect Dr Sankey doesn't get her own way this time. Now is my chance to do things my way and I want you dead. Either get in the boat or I shoot you now."

Savannah held her hands up. "Okay, okay." She stumbled to her feet, making it look harder than it was now her limbs were mostly back to normal. Her only chance was to try and get the gun from Darla.

She moved to lift her leg over the edge of the small wooden

rowboat on the bank of the river and felt Darla behind her. She stumbled on purpose and as Darla lurched forward, she went for the gun.

Darla held on as she tried to get a firm grip on the small woman who was freakishly strong, the gun between them, and then a loud pop filled the air. Savannah looked at Darla in shock as the gun went off.

Chapter Twenty-Five

"Lopez, I swear if you don't find her in the next thirty seconds, I'm going to lose my shit." Decker was pacing the tech room at Eidolon, each step filled with utter dread. He couldn't lose Savannah; he'd never recover.

Waggs laid a hand on his arm "Calm down. Let Lopez do his thing."

Decker shrugged it off as he turned on his friend. "Calm down? Are you fucking kidding me? If this was Willow, would you be calm?"

Waggs jaw clenched, and he raised one eyebrow clearly unimpressed. "This was Willow if you remember, and a good friend of mine told me the same thing. Losing your mind won't help us or her."

Decker felt his anger toward his friend dissipate. "I'm sorry, I just... I can't lose her."

"I know and we'll find her. Savannah is smart. She'll do what she needs to do until we can get to her."

"Got her!" Lopez shouted and Decker rushed to look over, Lopez's shoulder. He saw an image of Savannah saying goodbye to Addie around an hour earlier and then she went out of shot. Lopez picked her up on a different camera. A heavily pregnant woman came into view and his gut felt like it was filled with lead. Darla Jenkins approached Savannah and they seemed to have a conversation before Savannah went off with her.

"Do we have audio?" His frustration had him pacing again, his usual cool demeanour shot.

Lopez pointed at the second screen. "No, but I have her near the loading zone."

Decker watched as Savannah moved to the trunk of the car and Darla moved up behind her and Savannah seemed to collapse as Darla pushed her into the trunk and closed the lid.

"She drugged her after getting her to the car." His hands were in his hair now as he paced.

Jack strode in with Aubrey close behind him. "That's not all. Darla Jenkins isn't pregnant. She was but she lost the baby three weeks before Andy Farr was murdered. We pulled her medical notes, and it states she had a second-trimester miscarriage."

"Jesus, and she's still pretending she's pregnant?" Gunner, who'd been quiet until then, stated. "She must be in a bad way mentally."

"Yeah, so we need to move." Jack glanced at him and then Lopez. "Is the tracker on Darla's car still in place from when she was in protective custody?"

Lopez's fingers flew over the keyboard and in seconds the red blip flashed, giving them a location.

Decker leaned in close. "They're at Whitney-On-Wye."

Gunner leaned in behind him. "I know that spot. Kanan and I went kayaking there."

"Let's hustle," Jack called and the team of five men and one woman—him, Jack, Waggs, Gunner, Blake, and Aubrey—were out the door.

The twenty-minute drive was the longest of his life and he prayed like he hadn't since his son died that they'd be in time, that this time would be different. He tried to calm his mind and breathe. Savannah didn't need him losing his legendary calm now when she needed it most. She needed him to step up for her and that was exactly what he would do, there would be time to emotionally fail after she was safe.

Blake pulled in a hundred feet from the VW Golf that belonged to Darla and the team jumped out. They had no clue what they were walking into and on the ride over had loaded up with weapons and tactical clothing. Aubrey had also requested an ambulance but asked that they come in quiet so as not to spook Darla.

On silent feet, they ran toward the sounds of voices and the sounds of a scuffle. They all stilled as the air was filled with the unmistakable sound of a gunshot. His belly bottomed out and he was running with no thought for his own safety, he just needed to get to her.

He rounded the bend where a cobble stone beach led to the river and stopped dead. Savannah was standing over Darla, a gun in her hand, her body swaying slightly as she leaned back and grabbed for a small rowboat behind her to support her.

"Savannah!" He was running, his eyes moving over every inch of her body checking for injury.

"Mark?" Her voice was scratchy and weak as he got to her, his hands running over her to determine if the blood covering her abdomen was hers.

"Are you okay?"

"Yes. I..." Savannah stopped and looked down at Darla as Waggs and the team worked on the fallen woman. Savannah pulled from his hold and straightened as if pulling herself together she fell to her knees and began shouting instructions at the others, completely taking over the care of the woman who'd meant to harm her.

He watched in awe as she gave instructions to the paramedics and helped them stabilise Darla for transport to the hospital.

He wasn't feeling so forgiving and would happily have left her to die. He knew that wasn't really true, but it was how he felt as he watched the woman he loved work to save someone who'd done nothing but hateful things to her.

"We need to get her into theatre now."

He watched, feeling like a spare part, as Savannah climbed into the back of the ambulance with the crew. Her eyes came to him once, a look of loss on her beautiful face before the doors closed and the rig was driving away.

"Come on, Deck, I'll give you a lift to the hospital while Aubrey processes the scene. We don't want anyone else to see us here."

Jack urged him toward the SUV, and he followed, grateful. He didn't care if he couldn't see her, he needed to be close to her. He'd let far too much time pass without feeling her in his arms or seeing her, and he couldn't go any longer.

At the hospital, he was told that Darla Jenkins had been taken into theatre and another nurse told him Dr Sankey was performing the surgery. "Is that usual?"

"It is for a neuro procedure, where the bullet nicked her spine, yes."

He didn't ask more questions in case the nurse was unaware of the specifics, so he sat and waited in the second-floor hallway outside the theatre.

Addie handed him a coffee as the time rolled into the sixth hour. "Here, you look shattered."

"Thanks." He took it and sipped the fragrant liquid before leaning forward, elbows on his knees. "How is she, Addie, and tell me the truth?"

"Hurt, missing you, but doing okay. Savannah is strong and seeks the positives in life. She's been offered a job in Germany."

Decker closed his eyes against the feeling of panic at the thought he might be too late.

"She hasn't taken it yet, but she needs a reason to stay. Give her one."

"I love her."

"Then tell her that. Don't let fear steal a future that could be filled with beauty."

"What if it's too late?" His biggest fear was that he'd left it too long and she'd want nothing to do with him.

"Then you work harder until you convince her you're the man she fell in love with and you're sticking around."

Deck smiled as he glanced at Adeline. "Lopez struck gold when he found you."

"I think we both did."

"True."

"Want me to wait with you?"

"No, get home to your family. I'm going to wait until she gets out of surgery."

"Okay, Deck."

He watched Addie walk away thinking about what she'd said. He'd do whatever it took to convince Savannah that he was worth the risk with her heart and spend his life making up for his mistakes.

Five hours later, Savannah walked out of the operating theatre looking exhausted as she pulled the scrub cap off her head. He stood and walked toward her and saw her stop when she noticed him. "Savannah?"

"What are you doing here, Mark?"

"Can we talk?"

Savannah shook her head. "I can't right now. I have to give a statement to Aubrey and I'm dead on my feet. I need to go home and sleep."

"Will you let me drive you home?"

"Why?" She frowned looking confused and he knew he had an uphill climb on his hands.

"Because I need to know you're safe."

"Fine, whatever."

He smiled at the first small victory as he watched her walk away and resisted the urge to take her in his arms and hold her. He needed to be patient with her. He'd done damage with his words and actions and now he had to show her how sorry he was because words wouldn't be enough.

175

Two hours later, at almost two in the morning, he stopped outside Savannah's home and looked across at the woman who had slain his demons with her sweet nature and fiery determination. Her eyelashes fluttered against her cheeks as she woke from her catnap.

She pushed to sitting and blinked slowly. "Are we home already? I must have fallen asleep."

"Yeah, doc, we're home." He'd never felt more at peace than when he was with her. She *was* home to him. He didn't say the words though, she needed to sleep more than she needed his word vomit. She was almost cross-eyed with fatigue. He unclipped her seatbelt and walked her to her door, placing his hands in his pockets to keep from reaching for her.

She turned at the door and faced him. "Thanks for the ride, Deck."

He hated that she called him that now, that he'd made her raise barriers. He nodded. "When can I see you? We need to talk."

Savannah crossed her arms defensively over her chest and looked down at her crocs and the clean scrubs she'd worn home. Her hair was wild, and she had bags under her eyes, and he'd never seen her look more beautiful.

"I don't know, Deck."

"Mark." He lifted his hand and then dropped it before he touched her. "To you I'm Mark."

Savannah scowled. "Fine, *Mark*. I don't know when I'm free."

"What about tomorrow morning? We could get breakfast somewhere."

"Whatever, although I don't see the point."

"Please?"

"Okay, yes. Now can I please go to bed before I fall asleep at this door standing up?"

He grinned. "Sure thing, doc."

"Goodnight, Mark."

"Goodnight, doc."

As she closed the door, he heard her call. "And don't call me doc. I don't like it."

He grinned wider. "You love it."

He didn't catch the rest but that was okay. He'd see her tomorrow and it filled his heart with happiness.

Chapter Twenty-Six

A tapping on his car window had him sitting up with a start, the crisp early morning sun bright on the first day of October. He glanced at his window and saw Savannah standing there in her old UCLH hoodie, her arms crossed over her middle, this time not in defence but from the cold.

Her face looking irritated and confused as he pressed the button to lower the window. "Hey, doc."

"What the hell are you doing, Mark? It's seven am!"

He smirked. "Waiting to take you to breakfast."

"How long have you been out here?"

Deck grabbed the door handle and Savannah stepped back as he exited the car and stood, stretching his arms above his head. He saw her eyes travel over his body and linger where his tee rode up and exposed a patch of skin on his abdomen. Her eyes jumped guiltily to his and he winked, making her blush. Fuck, he'd missed her.

"Well, to answer your question now you've finished objectifying my body, Dr Sankey, I went home after I left here, showered and changed, and was back by four am."

"You're out of your mind."

"Perhaps."

Savannah stalked off, giving him a chance to admire her sexy ass in the tight jeans she loved to wear which fit like a second skin. She turned back and caught him ogling her and he grinned totally unrepentant.

"Get your ass in the house before my neighbours call the cops."

He jogged to catch up with her and followed her inside, closing her front door and taking in the space he'd missed. They'd spent so little time here, but it was filled with everything that encapsulated the woman he was in love with.

Savannah poured him a coffee and passed it to him.

"Thanks."

She brushed past him with her own cup on her way to the living room, sinking into her comfy chair and tucking her feet beneath her, all protective poses as she turned to face him, tucking her still wet hair behind her ears.

"So, what did you want to speak to me about? Seems we might as well get this over with now."

Her cool attitude was a front, but he still hated it because it wasn't her. She was an optimist, a positive person, not the negative unaffected woman she was showing him.

"I want to apologise for the things I said to you at my house. I was wrong and my words and actions were despicable. I didn't mean any of it and I'm truly sorry for hurting you."

He saw her look down at her mug as if she couldn't meet his eyes and he knew he needed to touch her.

He fell to his knees beside her chair and pried her hand from her mug so he could set it on the table. "Look at me, beautiful." Her wet eyes moved to him, and a pain tightened across his chest at the sight. "Fuck, doc." He drew her into his arms and held her tight, lifting her and setting her back down on his lap as he took her chair.

"I'm sorry, I'm just overwrought, that's all." She wiped at her tears and tried to climb off his lap, but he held her tight. "Let me go,

Mark." She wriggled and his dick hardened at the feel of her softness against his cock.

"No, I'm never letting you go again. I tried that and it was utter misery."

He saw a flicker of hope mixed with a hefty dose of trepidation on her pretty face.

"What are you saying?"

"What I should have said weeks ago." He brought his hands up to cup her face as her hands gripped his wrists. "I love you, Savannah. I'm so fucking in love with you, I can't breathe without you. I tried so hard to fight it, but you can't fight fate. You were made for me, and I was made for you. You're so much smarter than me because you saw it when I was still being a fucking idiot, but I see it now."

"You love me? But you love your wife. I can never be her and I won't be her substitute."

"I'll always love Susie, but she's gone. What I feel for you puts my love for Susie in the shade. I would never ask you to be anyone but you because you're perfect for me. Susie gave me Milo. For that and the time we shared, I'll always miss and love her but what I feel for you is indescribable. You're the air I need to breathe. I feel like I'm dying without you. You took a man who'd let all hope of a future go and filled him with life."

He kissed her nose, leaning his forehead against hers. "I want a life with you. I want to wake up with you in my arms, go to sleep at night with you knowing that whatever happens in our lives it will be okay because I have you. I want us to travel, build a home, have a family. I want it all with you because the thought of anything else is desolate and empty."

"You want all that with me?"

Decker smirked as he raised his head and saw her hope bloom to life. "Yes, I want it all. I love you. You're the smartest, sweetest, strongest, kindest, most beautiful human on the planet and I fucking love you."

"What if you change your mind?"

He closed his eyes knowing he deserved her mistrust. "I won't change my mind. I'd marry you right this second if I could."

Savannah laughed and it was the sweetest sound he'd ever heard. "Is that a proposal, Mark Decker?"

"If you want it to be. I'm so ready to start my life with you, Savannah."

"Well, you ain't getting off the hook that easy. I want romance, mister."

"Then romance is what you'll get. Now can I please kiss you? It feels like a lifetime since I tasted you."

"Kiss me, Mark."

"Thank fuck."

His head dipped and his lips crashed into hers and a storm of emotion flooded him. He angled her head, his tongue thrusting into her mouth as her hands ran through his hair, gripping hard and sending a bolt of lust straight through his body.

"It's been too long, Mark. I need you."

"Jesus Christ."

He stood, lifting her as her legs wrapped around his waist and his fingers flexed into the perfect curve of her ass. He took her stairs two at a time as if she weighed nothing, his body pinning her to the wall on the landing by her door. He couldn't get further without tasting her.

He let her legs drop as he kissed his way down her neck. "Fuck, I missed you doc."

"Hurry."

Her urgency was like an aphrodisiac, and he became unhinged. His hands tore at her clothes exposing the perfection of her body as she tugged at his shirt and helped free him from his jeans.

He dropped to his knees in front of her and kissed her hip bones before he looked up and saw the look of utter love and devotion mixed with naked desire on her face and he almost came right then and there.

A growl left his throat as he bent his head, hooked her leg over his shoulder, and found her wet and ready for him. He thrust two fingers inside her as his tongue teased her clit. Her hand slammed down on his head and her back arched against the wall. He worked her body, his own on the edge, his cock aching to be inside her again, but he wanted her to come first. He wasn't sure he'd last once he was inside her again.

"That's it, beautiful. Squeeze my fingers with that tight pussy." He felt her body clench, her breath coming in short gasps now.

"Oh God, oh fuck. I'm gonna come."

"Come all over my hand, Savannah."

His words sent her over and he felt her body grow taut before she was riding his face, desperate and wild and fucking perfect.

Her legs went slack, and he pulled away, the taste and scent of her all over his body. He felt marked, claimed, and it was beautiful. He stood, kissing her as he lifted her and stumbled into her room, dropping them both to the bed. His body nestled between her soft thighs, her wet pussy cushioning his hard cock.

He lifted up on his elbows, his arms either side of her head. He wanted to see her eyes when he claimed her. "I love you, Savannah."

His cock nudged inside her and she sighed, her back arching in pleasure as he groaned. She was better than perfection, she was fucking heaven sent. Her legs came up and locked around his waist as he slid deeper inside her, his cock rubbing against her G-spot. He made love to her as they kept eye contact, the connection forming that he knew nobody could break.

This was life-changing and he wanted it. He didn't fear the future any longer, he was excited for every single second of it with this woman. As their bodies rode the high of climax together, he didn't think his life could get any better but in the coming years, his Savannah would show him so much beauty that he'd learn better than to think he'd seen it all.

Epilogue

"Here, let me straighten your tie."

Savannah reached over to her handsome husband and straightened the already perfect tie. She smiled up at him as he smirked before wrapping his free hand around her hip and pulling her close for a kiss. Five years and still her need for this man flared with just a kiss or look.

A chubby hand landed on her cheek followed by a giggle, and she pulled away from Mark to look at her small son, sitting comfortably in his father's arms. Sebastian was the image of his father, from his dark hair to his brown eyes that were filled with mischief.

"Hey, Mister, why can't I kiss Mommy?" Mark tickled his son's belly making him giggle, causing Alex to turn around and grin at Sebastian and Mark.

"My Mommy."

"Yeah, well, she was mine first, buddy," Mark said with a wry grin.

A tug on her leg made her look down at Liza, their three-year-old daughter who was another one who looked like her dad, except she had her eyes. Where Seb was mischief, Liza was serious. Curious from the word go, she'd captured their hearts and moulded them, so she held them in her tiny hands.

It had been a beautiful thing to watch her heal Mark in ways she knew she'd never have been able to. Not that he needed it, he was all-in for their family since the day she'd let him back into her life. They'd married quickly and he'd followed her to Germany, stating he'd work remotely or travel, but he wanted her to have her dream.

She'd told him she had her dream in him, but he'd insisted he didn't want her to miss out and she'd loved her time at the Gesund-heit Institute. But when she got pregnant with Liza, she knew it was time to come home. She now ran the Gromadski Neuroscience Foundation set up in Percy's name, along with his husband.

It was a crazy busy life and with another baby on the way in six months, it was only going to get more so but she loved her life. If she could've planned it, she'd never have dreamed it would end up so perfect.

Mark kissed her cheek as the rest of the people in the room began to fall silent. The room was filled with everyone from the Eidolon team and their partners, and the many children they now had between them, as well as the Fortis and Zenobi teams and their families, it was a day of celebration. Today they'd watch as Jack and Will Granger were appointed the Knights of the Garter for their service to the Queen and Country.

The private chapel at Windsor Castle was stunning. Ornate stained-glass windows, carved arches, and scones in the roof, and black and white tile flooring. Magnificently carved oak choir stalls ran parallel to the aisle for the knights of the Order of the Garter, the highest order of Knighthood in Britain. Above the pews hung the banners of its members, along with the coats of arms of over 700 former members.

Savannah gripped Mark's hand tightly as the Queen and her husband, the Duke, walked down the aisle, with the Duke always one step behind his Queen. After hearing the many stories about these two from Astrid it was astonishing to see them again up close.

Decked out in feathers and ceremonial dress, Queen Lydia bestowed the highest honour imaginable on Jack and Will by commending them to this very select group. The history of the two families went back hundreds of years and was as strong now as it would always be. As Jack glanced back at a heavily pregnant Astrid, the Queen said something which made Jack laugh before smiling at his true queen, his wife.

Liza pointed up at the banners. "Daddy, what are those?"

Mark crouched to his daughter and lifted her into his other arm. "Each knight displays a banner or arms, a helmet, a crest, a sword, and an enamelled stall plate in St. George's Chapel. That's the banner of a brave Knight from hundreds of years ago."

"Will Uncle Jack and Uncle Will have that?"

"Yes, sweetheart, they will."

"Oh. Okay, Daddy."

Savannah smiled at Mark; her heart full of love before she faced the front again to watch Will take a knee beside Jack.

'*Honi soit qui mal y pense*' meaning, 'Shame on him who thinks this evil' rang loud and true throughout the hushed chapel as the Queen committed them to the order. Goosebumps ran through her at the majesty of the moment and more than one woman had tears in their eyes.

A man in full robes stepped forward and unrolled a beautiful scroll before he began to read from it.

"Alex Martinez, Calvin Blake, Kirk Reid, Liam Hayes, Mitchell Quinn, Gunner Ramberg, Aiden Wagner, Javier Lopez, and Mark Decker, please step forward."

Savannah smiled at her husband as he kissed her quickly and then made his way with the other men of Eidolon to the front alter where the Queen was seated on her throne.

Savannah watched as her husband was awarded a Knighthood, different to what Jack and Will had just received but no less worthy in her book. Mark looked dashing in a bespoke three-piece suit, which he only wore for special occasions now. The other men either wore suits or their military uniform.

Addie reached for her hand, the two friends looking on with pride as their husbands bent their knee and the sword was tapped to each shoulder. This private ceremony was unlike any other, as the secrecy of the team who protected the Monarch and her family and the connections they shared was still very much a privileged knowledge.

As Mark stood, his eyes coming to her, Savannah wiped a tear from her eye. He'd come a long way from the man who was determined never to love again. He now took every opportunity to show his love and affection, and not for one second did she regret her decision to forgive him. Loving him was never a choice but if it had been, it would've been the right one. He was the love of her life, and she was the luckiest woman alive to be loved by him and have the family they shared.

Epilogue Two

As he watched his youngest daughter dance with her new husband it was hard to understand where the time had gone. A life filled with the beauty his gorgeous Savannah had brought to his life. His eyes moved from Isla and the man he knew would take care of her as if she were the most precious person on the planet, to his own wife of twenty-five years.

Savannah, as she always did, sensed his eyes on her and lifted her head from where she was talking to Willow and Astrid, a smile creasing her lips. The mother of the groom followed her eye line and landed on the man who was standing next to him. The look of love in her eyes was as bright today as the day he'd watched them wed.

"Can you believe we're here, at our kids' wedding?"

Decker sipped the brandy from the crystal tumbler before he glanced at Jack. "Nope. Not sure when it happened but we grew up."

Jack snorted. "That we did, Deck, that we did."

Alex, Liam, Lopez, Mitch, Waggs, Blake, Reid, and Gunner joined them, all of them watching on as the happy couple gazed into each other's eyes. Deck could see the love Ethan had for Isla. He adored her as much as he himself did, and he knew there was nothing that young man wouldn't do to make his new wife happy. He'd given them a hard time at first before he realised nobody would ever be good enough for his baby girl. Ethan was a good man, and in all honesty, he couldn't have chosen a better man for her.

"He'll look after her, you know. He's loved her since the day they met."

Jack was a good man, and an even better friend and Decker didn't know where he'd be if he hadn't met him and changed the course of his life.

Slowly the women they loved drifted toward them. He took Savannah in his arms and kissed her as her familiar body, that he loved every bit as much today as he did the day he married her, pressed against him.

"They look beautiful, together, don't they?" Not for the first time today, he dabbed a tear from her eye.

"Not as beautiful as you."

She smiled, her cheeks going pink even after all these years together and batted his chest. "Behave."

"What? It's true. You're the most stunning woman in the room."

"I love you, Mark Decker."

"I love you too, Savannah Decker."

"A toast."

Liam began handing out glasses from a tray he'd grabbed from a passing waiter. All of their children were scattered about the room celebrating their friends' wedding.

Clara and Xiomara, Alex and Evelyn's daughters were talking with Liberty and Lana, who were Reid and Liam's daughters respectively. Alex's son, Luis was chatting up a woman in the corner, his model good looks like catnip to women.

Maggie was dancing with Rafe, Reid's oldest son while his younger son, Cruz, was talking with Blake's daughters, Ariella and Matilda. Liza, his oldest was laughing with the other two bridesmaids, Ember and Evangeline, Jack's two daughters and the women, along with Astrid, who'd softened the hardened leader of Eidolon.

That left the rest of the Eidolon kids, his boy Seb, Lopez's kids, Payton and Xavier, Waggs sons, AJ and Flynn, Mitch's son, Devon, and daughter, Bailee, Liam's oldest daughter, Nuha and Gunner's two girls, Wren and Harmoni, at the huge round table in the corner, laughing and drinking.

He grinned at Savannah and winked as her free hand curled into his. "What are we toasting now?"

"To friends that are family."

The group toasted and raised their glasses.

"To our children, and the future they hold in their hands." Jack raised his glass and again they toasted.

"To the next Eidolon wedding." Astrid laughed she looked towards Ember, who was being pulled onto the now full dance floor by their friend Zin Maklavoi's son, Maddox.

"Oh hell, no." Jack thrust his glass at Alex as he went to break up the smitten pair but was stopped by his wife.

"Jack Granger, don't you dare."

"But, firefly, he has a reputation."

"Ember can handle him."

"But..."

Deck was trying not to laugh as his friend struggled to convince his wife that Ember should be locked in a tower. "Not so funny now it's your daughter is it, Jack?"

Jack glared at him, and he laughed harder.

"You going to dance with me, handsome?"

He glanced at his wife who was the light of his life, his second chance and one he thanked God for every day. He'd been through hell and she and his family were his reward. "I sure am, doc."

She smiled as he led her onto the dance floor that was filled with his friends, his family, their children, and knew he had a lot to be thankful for and a lot to look forward to. The reins of Eidolon had been handed to Ethan. The next generation was solid and strong and full of men and women who had what it took to get the job done. Now and he and his friends were enjoying retirement, although no one ever fully retired from this type of job, and he looked forward to the next instalment of his bountiful life.

Eidolon Family Tree

Alex and Evelyn — Clara, Xiomara, and Luis
Blake and Pax — Ariella and Matilda
Reid and Callie — Rafe, Liberty, and Cruz
Liam and Taamira — Lana and Nuha
Mitch and Autumn — Maggie, Devon, and Bailee
Gunner and Lacey — Wren and Harmoni
Waggs and Willow — AJ and Flynn
Jack and Astrid — Ethan, Ember, and Evangeline
Lopez and Adeline — Payton and Xavier
Decker and Savannah — Sebastian, Liza, and Isla

Sneak Peek: Guarding Salvation (Unedited)
Coming January 2020

The wood crackled in the log fire of the pub as Bein, Titan, and Lotus walked up to the bar. The pub was quintessentially British, from the brass taps to beer mats on the wall and it was a comfort on a cold night like this one. Bein nodded at Bob, who was talking to a local at the other end of the wooden bar as he waved back, acknowledging them. He was starving and one of Bob's steak and ale pies with creamy mash was just what he needed tonight. His head was buried in the menu deciding if he was going to have extra chips on the side when he heard a voice.

"What can I get you?"

He looked up and was met with the best pair of tits he'd seen in a long time, but that was nothing compared with the face that greeted him when he dragged his eyes upwards. He quickly averted his gaze from the plain purple tee, which shouldn't be sexy but on this beauty should be damn illegal.

Her eyebrows raised and he realised he'd been staring so long he'd forgotten he question. "Sorry what?"

"What would you like to drink?"

"Oh, I'll have two pints of ale and pint of Bulmer's Original, please."

He watched her begin pulling the pints with the ease of someone who'd been doing it for a long time. His eyes skimmed over tight fitted jeans that complimented her arse to perfection to her flat boots, which had seen better days but weren't cheap, which meant she must've had money at some point.

She had long dark hair which had highlights of red through it when she moved her head and the firelight caught her just right. Startling jade green eyes and pale skin, and if he wasn't very much mistaken, an Irish accent that she was trying very hard to hide.

Closing the menu, now he concentrated on the woman who was moving around the bar with ease, but he noticed she never once turned her back on him or anyone else in the room. Fascinated, Bein took in her frame, which was still thin despite the curves which were all natural and not from some weird injections or filler.

Her eyes wouldn't meet his as she placed his drinks on the bar mat in front of him. She seemed shy, hesitant, hyper-aware of her surroundings. "That'll be ten pounds, fifty-seven pence, please."

Bein handed over a twenty and she quickly turned to the cash register to get his change, again keeping the door and the patrons in sight. Someone in the pub dropped a glass and as it smashed, she jumped out of her skin, her whole-body tensing, her terrified eyes moving to the door looking for escape before she realised what it was and visibly relaxed her shoulders.

She moved to hand him his change and he held his hand up. "Keep it, darlin."

"Are you sure? That's a lot."

"Yeah, you have a drink yourself."

"Thank you, that's very kind." Still, she didn't meet his eyes.

He watched her put the change in the tip jar which he knew would be shared about among the other members of staff at the end of the week. "You're not from around here are ya?"

She gave him a deer in the headlights look before dropping her eyes in a way that made his dick sit up and take notice. His thoughts immediately went to her on her knees looking up at him through those long sexy lashes in a submissive position. God, he needed to get laid, and soon, if he was fantasising about terrified barmaids.

"No. How do you know that?"

"Relax, darlin, I work at the search and rescue centre so know most people around these parts, plus this is my local and I certainly would've remembered a beauty like you."

Usually, he didn't have to work to get a woman interested but this one fell flat, and she just shook her head. "I need to get on."

She walked away to refill the crisps and he was left with so many questions about this woman. Only one person could answer them, and he was still busy yammering. That was the thing with Bob, he loved to gossip so much he was like an old woman.

Walking towards his friends he set the three pints down, handing Titan his cider and Lotus her ale. He sat down took a long pull on the pint and wiped the foam from his upper lip.

He saw his friends smirking and frowned. "What?"

Titan shrugged. "Nothing, just never seen you strike out before. It's refreshing."

"Fuck off, I didn't even flirt with her."

"Oh, you definitely flirted with her, and she shut your ass down." Lotus was trying not laugh louder.

"I wasn't giving her my A-game and anyway, she seems too shy for me. Plus she's hiding something and I don't need that kind of drama."

Titan held up his pint in salute. "Yep, totally get it, man."

Lotus was playing with a spare beer mat twirling it between her fingers as if it was a throwing star. "So, what are your thoughts on Hansen?"

"Honestly, I think this guy has gone to ground and until he pokes his head above the parapet we're on a hiding to nothing."

"I agree, but we have to try. This is personal for Jack and Eidolon after what he did to Astrid and Adeline. This dick deserves to die for what he's done. Plus, I owe Jack more than I can ever repay."

Bein didn't know the full story, just that Lotus had been involved with the wrong people and Jack had given her a second chance.

Titan sat back in his chair, folding his hands over his chest. "Jack gave me back my self-worth, and for that he'll always have my loyalty."

"I think we can all agree that Jack is the reason we're here and not washed-up dead or in jail, but this is going to be a long game of cat and mouse with Hansen, and we need to play smart not fast. See through the chaos, instead of allowing this prick to play us."

A movement to his right had him turning to see the new barmaid laughing with old man Johnson. He had to be as old as these fucking mountains and yet he was still out on the hills day and night checking his sheep that roamed free. Her laugh was deep and husky. Real, not fake and tinkly like some women who did it for attention.

It made him wonder what he'd said to get that reaction. She must have felt him looking because she glanced up and the spark between them arced across the room, leaving him aching to talk to her, to kiss her and feel her skin before she broke the connection and looked swiftly away. It was a strange reaction to someone he hardly knew and not one he'd had before. Chemistry was a strange thing and they clearly had it in spades.

Pre Order Guarding Salvation Now

Want a Free Short Story?

Sign up for Maddie's Newsletter using the link below and receive a free copy of the short story, Fortis: Where it all Began.

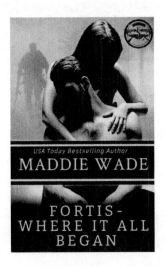

When hard-nosed SAS operator, Zack Cunningham is forced to work a mission with the fiery daughter of the American General, sparks fly. As those heated looks turn into scorching hot stolen kisses, a forbidden love affair begins that neither had expected.

Just as life is looking perfect disaster strikes and Ava Drake is left wondering if she will ever see the man she loves again.

https://dl.bookfunnel.com/cyrjtv3tta

Books by Maddie Wade

Fortis Security

Healing Danger (Dane and Lauren)

Stolen Dreams (Nate and Skye)

Love Divided (Jace and Lucy)

Secret Redemption (Zack and Ava)

Broken Butterfly (Zin and Celeste)

Arctic Fire (Kanan and Roz)

Phoenix Rising (Daniel and Megan)

Nate & Skye Wedding Novella

Digital Desire (Will and Aubrey)

Paradise Ties: A Fortis Wedding Novella (Jace and Lucy & Dane and Lauren)

Wounded Hearts (Drew and Mara)

Scarred Sunrise (Smithy and Lizzie)

Zin and Celeste: A Fortis Family Christmas

Fortis Boxset 1 (Books 1-3)

Fortis Boxset 2 (Books 4-7.5

* * *

Eidolon

Alex

Blake

Reid

Liam

Mitch

Gunner

Waggs

Jack

Lopez

Decker

* * *

Alliance Agency Series (co-written with India Kells)

Deadly Alliance

Knight Watch

Hidden Obsession

Lethal Justice

Innocent Target

Power Play

* * *

Ryoshi Delta (part of Susan Stoker's Police and Fire: Operation Alpha World)

Condor's Vow

Sandstorm's Promise

Hawk's Honor

Omega's Oath

* * *

Shadow Elite

Guarding Salvation

* * *

Tightrope Duet

Tightrope One

Tightrope Two

* * *

Angels of the Triad

01 Sariel

* * *

Other Worlds

Keeping Her Secrets *Suspenseful Seduction World* (Samantha A. Cole's World)

Finding English P*olice and Fire: Operation Alpha* (Susan Stoker's world)

About the Author

Contact Me

If stalking an author is your thing and I sure hope it is then here are the links to my social media pages.

If you prefer your stalking to be more intimate, then my group Maddie's Minxes will welcome you with open arms.

General Email: info.maddiewade@gmail.com
Email: maddie@maddiewadeauthor.co.uk
Website: http://www.maddiewadeauthor.co.uk
Facebook page: https://www.facebook.com/maddieuk/
Facebook group: https://www.facebook.com/
groups/546325035557882/
Amazon Author page: amazon.com/author/maddiewade
Goodreads:
https://www.goodreads.com/author/show/14854265.Maddie_Wade
Bookbub: https://partners.bookbub.com/authors/3711690/edit
Twitter: @mwadeauthor
Pinterest: @maddie_wade
Instagram: Maddie Author

Printed in Great Britain
by Amazon

11061478R00122